NOW BUT NOT YET

ETERNITY NOW: VOLUME 5

NOW BUT NOT YET

JOHN

THOMAS NELSON
Since 1798

www.ThomasNelson.com

NET NT Series Eternity Now: *Volume 5: Now But Not Yet*

Published in Nashville, Tennessee, by Thomas Nelson. Thomas Nelson is a registered trademark of HarperCollins Christian Publishing, Inc.

For free access to the NET Bible, the complete set of 60,000 translators' notes, and Bible study resources, visit:

bible.org
netbible.org
netbible.com

Library of Congress Control Number: 2021952034

This Bible was set in the Thomas Nelson NET Typeface, created at the 2K/DENMARK A/S type foundry.

Printed in the United States of America

22 23 24 25 25 27 28 29 30 / TRM / 10 9 8 7 6 5 4 3 2 1

CONTENTS

TO THE READER

AN INTRODUCTION TO THE NEW ENGLISH TRANSLATION

You have been born anew . . . through the living and enduring word of God.
1 Peter 1:23

The New English Translation (NET) is the newest complete translation of the original biblical languages into English. In 1995 a multidenominational team of more than twenty-five of the world's foremost biblical scholars gathered around the shared vision of creating an English Bible translation that could overcome old challenges and boldly open the door for new possibilities. The translators completed the first edition in 2001 and incorporated revisions based on scholarly and user feedback in 2003 and 2005. In 2019 a major update reached its final stages. The NET's unique translation process has yielded a beautiful, faithful English Bible for the worldwide church today.

What sets the NET Bible apart from other translations? We encourage you to read the full story of the NET's development and additional details about its translation philosophy at netbible.com/net-bible-preface. But we would like to draw your attention to a few features that commend the NET to all readers of the Word.

TRANSPARENT AND ACCOUNTABLE

Have you ever wished you could look over a Bible translator's shoulder as he or she worked?

Bible translation usually happens behind closed doors—few outside the translation committee see the complex decisions underlying the words that appear in their English Bibles. Fewer still have the opportunity to review and speak into the translators' decisions.

Throughout the NET's translation process, every working draft was made publicly available on the Internet. Bible scholars, ministers, and laypersons from around the world logged millions of review sessions. No other translation is so openly accountable to the worldwide church or has been so thoroughly vetted.

And yet the ultimate accountability was to the biblical text itself. The NET Bible is neither crowdsourced nor a "translation by consensus." Rather, the NET translators filtered every question and suggestion through the very best insights from biblical linguistics, textual criticism, and their unswerving commitment to following the text wherever it leads. Thus, the NET remains supremely accurate and trustworthy while also benefiting from extensive review by those who would be reading, studying, and teaching from its pages.

BEYOND THE "READABLE VS. ACCURATE" DIVIDE

The uniquely transparent and accountable translation process of the NET has been crystallized in the most extensive set of Bible translators' notes ever created. More than 60,000 notes highlight every major decision, outline alternative views, and explain difficult or nontraditional renderings. Freely available at netbible.org and in print in the *NET Bible, Full Notes Edition*, these notes help the NET overcome one of the biggest challenges facing any Bible translation: the tension between *accuracy* and *readability*.

If you have spent more than a few minutes researching the English version of the Bible, you have probably encountered a "translation spectrum"—a simple chart with the most wooden-but-precise translations and paraphrases on the far left (representing a "word-for-word" translation approach) and the loosest-but-easiest-to-read translations and paraphrases on the far right (representing a "thought-for-thought" philosophy of translation). Some translations intentionally lean toward one end of the spectrum or the other, embracing the strengths and weaknesses of their chosen approach. Most try to strike a balance between the extremes, weighing accuracy against readability—striving to reflect the grammar of the underlying biblical languages while still achieving acceptable English style.

But the NET moves beyond that old dichotomy. Because of the extensive translators' notes, the NET never has to compromise. Whenever faced with a difficult translation choice, the translators were free to put the strongest option in the main text while documenting the challenge, their thought process, and the solution in the notes.

The benefit to you, the reader? You can be sure that the NET is a translation you can trust—nothing has been lost in translation or obscured by a translator's dilemma. Instead, you are invited to see for yourself and gain the kind of transparent access to the biblical languages previously available only to scholars.

MINISTRY FIRST

One more reason to love the NET: Modern Bible translations are typically copyrighted, posing a challenge for ministries hoping to quote more than a few passages in their Bible study resources, curriculum, or other programming. But the NET is for everyone, with "ministry first" copyright innovations that encourage ministries to quote and share the life-changing message of Scripture as freely as possible. In fact, one of the major motivations behind the creation of the NET was the desire to ensure that ministries had unfettered access to a top-quality modern Bible translation without needing to embark on a complicated process of securing permissions.

Visit netbible.com/net-bible-copyright to learn more.

TAKE UP AND READ

With its balanced, easy-to-understand English text and a transparent translation process that invites you to see for yourself the richness of the biblical languages, the NET is a Bible you can embrace as your own. Clear, readable, elegant, and accurate, the NET presents Scripture as meaningfully and powerfully today as when these words were first communicated to the people of God.

Our prayer is that the NET will be a fresh and exciting invitation to you—and Bible readers everywhere—to "let the word of Christ dwell in you richly" (Col 3:16).

The Publishers

JOHN

PROLOGUE

John was a fisherman by trade, which meant he spent hours studying the waters. Where did the fish gather? What weather conditions brought them closer to the surface? When was the best time to catch them? John's goal was to remove as much of the guesswork from fishing as possible. It wasn't enough to *hope* he would catch fish; he needed to *know* he would. His livelihood depended on it.

Then one day, John's life changed for good. A traveling teacher in the region named Jesus called out two simple words to him: "Follow me." In that instant, John had to decide. Did he accept this invitation from a man he didn't really know? Was he willing to walk away from life as he knew it? To leave fishing—and his family—behind? It made no sense, but as John contemplated the offer, he knew he had made his decision when his hands dropped the fishing nets he was working on. He would follow Jesus.

Soon John realized that he had looked at Jesus' offer all wrong. Choosing to leave everything behind to follow Jesus was actually a sensible decision. *Not* following Jesus would have made no sense. John had given up much, but in Jesus he had come to know something that mattered much more.

CHAPTER 1

THE PROLOGUE TO THE GOSPEL

In the beginning was the Word, and the Word was with God, and the Word was fully God. The Word was with God in the beginning. All things were created by him, and apart from him not one thing was created that has been created. *In him was life,* and the life was the light of mankind. And the light shines on in the darkness, but the darkness has not mastered it.

A man came, sent from God, whose name was John. He came as a witness to testify about the light, so that everyone might believe through him. He himself was not the light, but he came to testify about the light. The true light, who gives light to everyone, was coming into the world. He was in the world, and the world was created by him, but the world did not recognize him. He came to what was his own, but his own people did not receive him. But to all who have received him—those who believe in his name—he has given the right to become God's children—children not born by human parents or by human desire or a husband's decision, but by God.

Now the Word became flesh and took up residence among us. We saw his glory—the glory of the one and only, full of grace and truth, who came from the Father. John testified about him and shouted out, "This one was the one about whom I said, 'He who comes after me is greater than I am, because he existed before me.'" For we have all received from his fullness one gracious gift after another. For the law was given through Moses, but grace and truth came about through Jesus Christ. No one has ever seen God. The only one, himself God, who is in closest fellowship with the Father, has made God known.

THE TESTIMONY OF JOHN THE BAPTIST

Now this was John's testimony when the Jewish leaders sent priests and Levites from Jerusalem to ask him, "Who are you?" He confessed—he did not deny but confessed—"I am not the Christ!" So they asked him, "Then who are you? Are you Elijah?" He said, "I am not!" "Are you the Prophet?" He answered, "No!" Then they said to him, "Who are you? Tell us so that we can give an answer to those who sent us. What do you say about yourself?"

John said, "I am ***the voice of one shouting in the wilderness, 'Make straight the way for the Lord,'*** as the prophet Isaiah said." (Now they had been sent from the Pharisees.) So they asked John, "Why then are you baptizing if you are not the Christ, nor Elijah, nor the Prophet?"

John answered them, "I baptize with water.

Among you stands one whom you do not recognize, who is coming after me. I am not worthy to untie the strap of his sandal!" These things happened in Bethany across the Jordan River where John was baptizing.

On the next day John saw Jesus coming toward him and said, "Look, the Lamb of God who takes away the sin of the world! This is the one about whom I said, 'After me comes a man who is greater than I am, because he existed before me.' I did not recognize him, but I came baptizing with water so that he could be revealed to Israel."

Then John testified, "I saw the Spirit descending like a dove from heaven, and it remained on him. And I did not recognize him, but the one who sent me to baptize with water said to me, 'The one on whom you see the Spirit descending and remaining—this is the one who baptizes with the Holy Spirit.' I have both seen and testified that this man is the Chosen One of God."

Again the next day John was standing there with two of his disciples. Gazing at Jesus as he walked by, he said, "Look, the Lamb of God!" When John's two disciples heard him say this, they followed Jesus. Jesus turned around and saw them following and said to them, "What do you want?" So they said to him, "Rabbi" (which is translated Teacher), "where are you staying?" Jesus answered, "Come and you will see." So they came and saw where he was staying, and they stayed with him that day. Now it was about four o'clock in the afternoon.

ANDREW'S DECLARATION

Andrew, the brother of Simon Peter, was one of the two disciples who heard what John said and followed Jesus. He first found his own brother Simon and told him, "We have found the Messiah!" (which is translated Christ). Andrew brought Simon to Jesus. Jesus looked at him and said, "You are Simon, the son of John. You will be called Cephas" (which is translated Peter).

THE CALLING OF MORE DISCIPLES

On the next day Jesus wanted to set out for Galilee. He found Philip and said to him, "Follow me." (Now Philip was from Bethsaida, the town of Andrew and Peter.) Philip found Nathanael and told him, "We have found the one Moses wrote about in the law, and the prophets also wrote about—Jesus of Nazareth, the son of Joseph." Nathanael replied, "Can anything good come out of Nazareth?" Philip replied, "Come and see."

Jesus saw Nathanael coming toward him and exclaimed, "Look, a true Israelite *in whom there is no deceit!*" Nathanael asked him, "How do you know me?" Jesus replied, "Before Philip called you, when you were under the fig tree, I saw you." Nathanael answered him, "Rabbi, you are the Son of God; you are the king of Israel!" Jesus said to him, "Because I told you that I saw you under the fig tree, do you believe? You will see greater things than these." He continued, "I tell all of you the solemn truth—you will see heaven opened and the angels of God ascending and descending on the Son of Man."

CHAPTER 2

TURNING WATER INTO WINE

Now on the third day there was a wedding at Cana in Galilee. Jesus' mother was there, and Jesus and his disciples were also invited to the wedding. When the wine ran out, Jesus' mother said to him, "They have no wine left." Jesus replied, "Woman, why are you saying this to me? My time has not yet come." His mother told the servants, "Whatever he tells you, do it."

Now there were six stone water jars there for Jewish ceremonial washing, each holding 20 or 30 gallons. Jesus told the servants, "Fill the water jars with water." So they filled them up to the very top. Then he told them, "Now draw some out and take it to the head steward," and they did. When the head steward tasted the water that had been turned to wine, not knowing where it came from (though the servants who had drawn the water knew), he called the bridegroom and said to him, "Everyone serves the good wine first, and then the cheaper wine when the guests are drunk. You have kept the good wine until now!" Jesus did this as the first of his miraculous signs, in Cana of Galilee. In this way he revealed his glory, and his disciples believed in him.

CLEANSING THE TEMPLE

After this he went down to Capernaum with his mother and brothers and his disciples, and they stayed there a few days. Now the Jewish Feast of Passover was near, so Jesus went up to Jerusalem.

He found in the temple courts those who were selling oxen and sheep and doves, and the money changers sitting at tables. So he made a whip of cords and drove them all out of the temple courts, with the sheep and the oxen. He scattered the coins of the money changers and overturned their tables. To those who sold the doves he said, "Take these things away from here! Do not make my Father's house a marketplace!" His disciples remembered that it was written, "***Zeal for your house will devour me.***"

So then the Jewish leaders responded, "What sign can you show us, since you are doing these things?" Jesus replied, "Destroy this temple and in three days I will raise it up again." Then the Jewish leaders said to him, "This temple has been under construction for 46 years, and are you going to raise it up in three days?" But Jesus was speaking about the temple of his body. So after he was raised from the dead, his disciples remembered that he had said this, and they believed the scripture and the saying that Jesus had spoken.

JESUS AT THE PASSOVER FEAST

Now while Jesus was in Jerusalem at the Feast of the Passover, many people believed in his name because they saw the miraculous signs he was doing. But Jesus would not entrust himself to them because he knew all people. He did not need anyone to testify about man, for he knew what was in man.

CHAPTER 3

CONVERSATION WITH NICODEMUS

Now a certain man, a Pharisee named Nicodemus, who was a member of the Jewish ruling council, came to Jesus at night and said to him, "Rabbi, we know that you are a teacher who has come from God. For no one could perform the miraculous signs that you do unless God is with him." Jesus replied, "I tell you the solemn truth, unless a person is born from above, he cannot see the kingdom of God." Nicodemus said to him, "How can a man be born when he is old? He cannot enter his mother's womb and be born a second time, can he?"

Jesus answered, "I tell you the solemn truth, unless a person is born of water and spirit, he cannot enter the kingdom of God. What is born of the flesh is flesh, and what is born of the Spirit is spirit. Do not be amazed that I said to you, 'You must all be born from above.' The wind blows wherever it will, and you hear the sound it makes, but do not know where it comes from and where it is going. So it is with everyone who is born of the Spirit."

Nicodemus replied, "How can these things be?" Jesus answered, "Are you the teacher of

Israel and yet you don't understand these things? I tell you the solemn truth, we speak about what we know and testify about what we have seen, but you people do not accept our testimony. If I have told you people about earthly things and you don't believe, how will you believe if I tell you about heavenly things? No one has ascended into heaven except the one who descended from heaven—the Son of Man. Just as Moses *lifted up the serpent in the wilderness,* so must the Son of Man be lifted up, so that everyone who believes in him may have eternal life."

For this is the way God loved the world: He gave his one and only Son, so that everyone who believes in him will not perish but have eternal life. For God did not send his Son into the world to condemn the world, but that the world should be saved through him. The one who believes in him is not condemned. The one who does not believe has been condemned already, because he has not believed in the name of the one and only Son of God. Now this is the basis for judging: that the light has come into the world and people loved the darkness rather than the light because their deeds were evil. For everyone who does evil deeds hates the light and does not come to the light, so that their deeds will not be exposed. But the one who practices the truth comes to the light, so that it may be plainly evident that his deeds have been done in God.

FURTHER TESTIMONY ABOUT JESUS BY JOHN THE BAPTIST

After this, Jesus and his disciples came into Judean territory, and there he spent time with them and was baptizing. John was also baptizing at Aenon near Salim because water was plentiful there, and people were coming to him and being baptized. (For John had not yet been thrown into prison.)

Now a dispute came about between some of John's disciples and a certain Jew concerning ceremonial washing. So they came to John and said to him, "Rabbi, the one who was with you on the other side of the Jordan River, about whom you testified—see, he is baptizing, and everyone is flocking to him!"

John replied, "No one can receive anything unless it has been given to him from heaven. You yourselves can testify that I said, 'I am not the Christ,' but rather, 'I have been sent before him.' The one who has the bride is the bridegroom. The friend of the bridegroom, who stands by and listens for him, rejoices greatly when he hears the bridegroom's voice. This then is my joy, and it is complete. He must become more important while I become less important."

The one who comes from above is superior to all. The one who is from the earth belongs to the earth and speaks about earthly things. The one who comes from heaven is superior to all. He testifies about what he has seen and heard, but no one accepts his testimony. The one who has accepted his testimony has confirmed clearly that God is truthful. For the one whom God has sent speaks the words of God, for he does not give the Spirit sparingly. The Father loves the Son and has placed all things under his authority. The one who believes in the Son has eternal life. The one who rejects the Son will not see life, but God's wrath remains on him.

CHAPTER 4

DEPARTURE FROM JUDEA

Now when Jesus knew that the Pharisees had heard that he was winning and baptizing more disciples than John (although Jesus himself was not baptizing, but his disciples were), he left Judea and set out once more for Galilee.

CONVERSATION WITH A SAMARITAN WOMAN

But he had to pass through Samaria. Now he came to a Samaritan town called Sychar, near the plot of land that Jacob had given to his son Joseph. Jacob's well was there, so Jesus, since he was tired from the journey, sat right down beside the well. It was about noon.

A Samaritan woman came to draw water. Jesus said to her, "Give me some water to drink." (For his disciples had gone off into the town to buy supplies.) So the Samaritan woman said to him, "How can you—a Jew—ask me, a Samaritan woman, for water to drink?" (For Jews use nothing in common with Samaritans.)

Jesus answered her, "If you had known the gift of God and who it is who said to you, 'Give me some water to drink,' you would have asked him, and he would have given you living water." "Sir," the woman said to him, "you have no bucket and the well is deep; where then do you get this living water? Surely you're not greater than our ancestor Jacob, are you? For he gave us this well and drank from it himself, along with his sons and his livestock."

Jesus replied, "Everyone who drinks some of this water will be thirsty again. But whoever drinks some of the water that I will give him will never be thirsty again, but the water that I will give him will become in him a fountain of water springing up to eternal life." The woman said to him, "Sir, give me this water, so that I will not be thirsty or have to come here to draw water." He said to her, "Go call your husband and come back here." The woman replied, "I have no husband." Jesus said to her, "Right you are when you said, 'I have no husband,' for you have had five husbands, and the man you are living with now is not your husband. This you said truthfully!"

The woman said to him, "Sir, I see that you are a prophet. Our fathers worshiped on this mountain, and you people say that the place where people must worship is in Jerusalem." Jesus said to her, "Believe me, woman, a time is coming when you will worship the Father neither on this mountain nor in Jerusalem.

You people worship what you do not know. We worship what we know because salvation is from the Jews. But a time is coming—and now is here—when the true worshipers will worship the Father in spirit and truth, for the Father seeks such people to be his worshipers. God is spirit, and the people who worship him must worship in spirit and truth." The woman said to him, "I know that Messiah is coming" (the one called Christ); "whenever he comes, he will tell us everything." Jesus said to her, "I, the one speaking to you, am he."

THE DISCIPLES RETURN

Now at that very moment his disciples came back. They were shocked because he was speaking with a woman. However, no one said, "What do you want?" or "Why are you speaking with her?" Then the woman left her water jar, went off into the town and said to the people, "Come, see a man who told me everything I ever did. Surely he can't be the Messiah, can he?" So they left the town and began coming to him.

WORKERS FOR THE HARVEST

Meanwhile the disciples were urging him, "Rabbi, eat something." But he said to them, "I have food to eat that you know nothing about." So the disciples began to say to one another, "No one brought him anything to eat, did they?" Jesus said to them, "My food is to do the will of the one who sent me and to complete his work. Don't you say, 'There are four more months and then comes the harvest?' I tell you, look up and see that the fields are already white for harvest! The one who reaps receives pay and gathers fruit for eternal life, so that the one who sows and the one who reaps can rejoice together. For in this instance the saying is true, 'One sows and another reaps.' I sent you to reap what you did not work for; others have labored and you have entered into their labor."

THE SAMARITANS RESPOND

Now many Samaritans from that town believed in him because of the report of the woman who testified, "He told me everything I ever did." So when the Samaritans came to him, they began asking him to stay with them. He stayed there two days, and because of his word many more believed. They said to the woman, "No longer do we believe because of your words, for we have heard for ourselves, and we know that this one really is the Savior of the world."

ONWARD TO GALILEE

After the two days he departed from there to Galilee. (For Jesus himself had testified that a prophet has no honor in his own country.) So when he came to Galilee, the Galileans welcomed him because they had seen all the things he had done in Jerusalem at the feast (for they themselves had gone to the feast).

HEALING THE ROYAL OFFICIAL'S SON

Now he came again to Cana in Galilee where he had made the water wine. In Capernaum there was a certain royal official whose son was sick. When he heard that Jesus had come back from Judea to Galilee, he went to him and begged him to come down and heal his son, who was about to die. So Jesus said to him, "Unless you people see signs and wonders you will never believe!" "Sir," the official said to him, "come down before my child dies." Jesus told him, "Go home; your son will live." The man believed the word that Jesus spoke to him, and set off for home.

While he was on his way down, his slaves met him and told him that his son was going to live. So he asked them the time when his condition began to improve, and they told him, "Yesterday at one o'clock in the afternoon the fever left him." Then the father realized that it was the very time Jesus had said to him, "Your son will live," and he himself believed along with his entire household. Jesus did this as his second miraculous sign when he returned from Judea to Galilee.

CHAPTER 5

HEALING A PARALYTIC AT THE POOL OF BETHESDA

After this there was a Jewish feast, and Jesus went up to Jerusalem. Now there is in Jerusalem by the Sheep Gate a pool called *Bethzatha* in Aramaic, which has five covered walkways. A great number of sick, blind, lame, and paralyzed people were lying in these walkways. Now a man was there who had been disabled for 38 years. When Jesus saw him lying there and when he realized that the man had been disabled a long time already, he said to him, "Do you want to become well?" The sick man answered him, "Sir, I have no one to put me into the pool when the water is stirred up. While I am trying to get into the water, someone else goes down there before me." Jesus said to him, "Stand up! Pick up your mat and walk." Immediately the man was healed, and he picked up his mat and started walking. (Now that day was a Sabbath.)

So the Jewish leaders said to the man who had been healed, "It is the Sabbath, and you are not permitted to carry your mat." But he answered them, "The man who made me well said to me, 'Pick up your mat and walk.' " They asked him, "Who is the man who said to you, 'Pick up your mat and walk'?" But the man who had been healed did not know who it was, for Jesus had slipped out, since there was a crowd in that place.

After this Jesus found him at the temple and said to him, "Look, you have become well. Don't sin any more, lest anything worse happen to you." The man went away and informed the Jewish leaders that Jesus was the one who had made him well.

RESPONDING TO JEWISH LEADERS

Now because Jesus was doing these things on the Sabbath, the Jewish leaders began persecuting him. So he told them, "My Father is working until now, and I too am working." For this reason the Jewish leaders were trying even harder to kill him because not only was he breaking the Sabbath, but he was also calling God his own Father, thus making himself equal with God.

So Jesus answered them, "I tell you the solemn truth, the Son can do nothing on his own initiative, but only what he sees the Father doing. For whatever the Father does, the Son does likewise. For the Father loves the Son and shows him everything he does, and will show him greater deeds than these, so that you will be amazed. For just as the Father raises the dead and gives them life, so also the Son gives life to whomever he wishes. Furthermore, the Father does not judge anyone, but has assigned all judgment to the Son, so that all people will honor the Son just as they honor the Father. The one who does not honor the Son does not honor the Father who sent him.

"I tell you the solemn truth, the one who hears my message and believes the one who sent me has eternal life and will not be condemned, but has crossed over from death to life. I tell you the solemn truth, a time is coming—and is now here—when the dead will hear the voice of the Son of God, and those who hear will live. For just as the Father has life in himself, thus he has granted the Son to have life in himself, and he has granted the Son authority to execute judgment because he is the Son of Man.

"Do not be amazed at this because a time is coming when all who are in the tombs will hear his voice and will come out—the ones who have done what is good to the resurrection resulting in life, and the ones who have done what is evil to the resurrection resulting in condemnation. I can do nothing on my own initiative. Just as I hear, I judge, and my judgment is just because I do not seek my own will, but the will of the one who sent me.

MORE TESTIMONY ABOUT JESUS

"If I testify about myself, my testimony is not true. There is another who testifies about me, and I know the testimony he testifies about me is true. You have sent to John, and he has testified to the truth. (I do not accept human testimony, but I say this so that you may be saved.) He was a lamp that was burning and shining, and you wanted to rejoice greatly for a short time in his light.

"But I have a testimony greater than that from John. For the deeds that the Father has assigned me to complete—the deeds I am now doing—testify about me that the Father has sent me. And the Father who sent me has himself testified about me. You people have never heard his voice nor seen his form at any time, nor do you have his word residing in you because you do not believe the one whom he sent. You study the scriptures thoroughly because you think in them you possess eternal life, and it is these same scriptures that testify about me, but you are not willing to come to me so that you may have life.

"I do not accept praise from people, but I know you, that you do not have the love of God within you. I have come in my Father's name, and you do not accept me. If someone else comes in his own name, you will accept him. How can you believe, if you accept praise from one another and don't seek the praise that comes from the only God?

"Do not suppose that I will accuse you before the Father. The one who accuses you is Moses, in whom you have placed your hope. If you believed Moses, you would believe me because he wrote about me. But if you do not believe what Moses wrote, how will you believe my words?"

CHAPTER 6

THE FEEDING OF THE 5,000

After this Jesus went away to the other side of the Sea of Galilee (also called the Sea of Tiberias). A large crowd was following him because they were observing the miraculous signs he was performing on the sick. So Jesus went on up the mountainside and sat down there with his disciples. (Now the Jewish Feast of the Passover was near.) Then Jesus, when he looked up and saw that a large crowd was coming to him, said to Philip, "Where can we buy bread so that these people may eat?" (Now Jesus said this to test him, for he knew what he was going to do.) Philip replied, "200 silver coins worth of bread would not be enough for them, for each one to get a little." One of Jesus' disciples, Andrew, Simon Peter's brother, said to him, "Here is a boy who has five barley loaves and two fish, but what good are these for so many people?"

Jesus said, "Have the people sit down." (Now there was a lot of grass in that place.) So the men sat down, about 5,000 in number. Then Jesus took the loaves, and when he had given thanks, he distributed the bread to those who were seated. He then did the same with the fish, as much as they wanted. When they were all satisfied, Jesus said to his disciples, "Gather up the broken pieces that are left over, so that nothing is wasted." So they gathered them up and filled 12 baskets with broken pieces from the five barley loaves left over by the people who had eaten.

Now when the people saw the miraculous sign that Jesus performed, they began to say to one another, "This is certainly *the Prophet who is to come into the world.*" Then Jesus, because he knew they were going to come and seize him by force to make him king, withdrew again up the mountainside alone.

WALKING ON WATER

Now when evening came, his disciples went down to the lake, got into a boat, and started to cross the lake to Capernaum. (It had already become dark, and Jesus had not yet come to them.) By now a strong wind was blowing and the sea was getting rough. Then, when they had rowed about three or four miles, they caught sight of Jesus walking on the lake, approaching the boat, and they were frightened. But he said to them, "It is I. Do not be afraid." Then they wanted to take him into the boat, and immediately the boat came to the land where they had been heading.

The next day the crowd that remained on the other side of the lake realized that only one small boat had been there, and that Jesus had not boarded it with his disciples, but that his disciples had gone away alone. Other boats from Tiberias came to shore near the place where they had eaten the bread after the Lord had given thanks. So when the crowd realized that neither Jesus nor his disciples were there, they got into the boats and came to Capernaum looking for Jesus.

JESUS' DISCOURSE ABOUT THE BREAD OF LIFE

When they found him on the other side of the lake, they said to him, "Rabbi, when did you get here?" Jesus replied, "I tell you the solemn truth, you are looking for me not because you saw miraculous signs, but because you ate all the loaves of bread you wanted. Do not work for the food that disappears, but for the food that remains to eternal life—the food which the Son of Man will give to you. For God the Father has put his seal of approval on him."

So then they said to him, "What must we do to accomplish the deeds God requires?" Jesus replied, "This is the deed God requires—to believe in the one whom he sent." So they said to him, "Then what miraculous sign will you perform, so that we may see it and believe you? What will you do? Our ancestors ate the manna in the wilderness, just as it is written, '***He gave them bread from heaven to eat.***' "

Then Jesus told them, "I tell you the solemn truth, it is not Moses who has given you the bread from heaven, but my Father is giving you the true bread from heaven. For the bread of God is the one who comes down from heaven and gives life to the world." So they said to him, "Sir, give us this bread all the time!"

Jesus said to them, "I am the bread of life. The one who comes to me will never go hungry, and the one who believes in me will never be thirsty. But I told you that you have seen me and still do not believe. Everyone whom the Father gives me will come to me, and the one who comes to me I will never send away. For I have come down from heaven not to do my own will but the will of the one who sent me. Now this is the will of the one who sent me—that I should not lose one person of every one he has given me, but raise them all up at the last day. For this is the will of my Father—for everyone who looks on the Son and believes in him to have eternal life, and I will raise him up at the last day."

Then the Jews who were hostile to Jesus began complaining about him because he said, "I am the bread that came down from heaven," and they said, "Isn't this Jesus the son of Joseph, whose father and mother we know? How can he now say, 'I have come down from heaven'?" Jesus replied, "Do not complain about me to one another. No one can come to me unless the Father who sent me draws him, and I will raise him up at the last day. It is written in the prophets, ***'And they will all be taught by God.'*** Everyone who hears and learns from the Father comes to me. (Not that anyone has seen the Father except the one who is from God—he has seen the Father.) I tell you the solemn truth, the one who believes has eternal life. I am the bread of life. Your ancestors ate the manna in the wilderness, and they died. This is the bread that has come down from heaven, so that a person may eat from it and not die. I am the living bread that came down from heaven. If anyone eats from this bread he will live forever. The bread that I will give for the life of the world is my flesh."

Then the Jews who were hostile to Jesus began to argue with one another, "How can this man give us his flesh to eat?" Jesus said to them, "I tell you the solemn truth, unless you eat the flesh of the Son of Man and drink his blood, you have no life in yourselves. The one who eats my flesh and drinks my blood has eternal life, and I will raise him up on the last day. For my flesh is true food, and my blood is true drink. The one who eats my flesh and drinks my blood resides in me, and I in him. Just as the living Father sent me, and I live because of the Father, so the one who consumes me will live because of me. This is the bread that came down from heaven; it is not like the bread your ancestors ate, but then later died. The one who eats this bread will live forever."

MANY FOLLOWERS DEPART

Jesus said these things while he was teaching in the synagogue in Capernaum. Then many of his disciples, when they heard these things, said, "This is a difficult saying! Who can understand it?" When Jesus was aware that his disciples were complaining about this, he said to them, "Does this cause you to be offended? Then what if you see the Son of Man ascending where he was before? The Spirit is the one who gives life; human nature is of no help! The words that I have spoken to you are spirit and are life. But there are some of you who do not believe." (For Jesus had already known from the beginning who those were who did not believe, and who it was who would betray him.) So Jesus added, "Because of this I told you that no one can come to me unless the Father has allowed him to come."

PETER'S CONFESSION

After this many of his disciples quit following him and did not accompany him any longer. So Jesus said to the twelve, "You don't want to go away too, do you?" Simon Peter answered him, "Lord, to whom would we go? You have the words of eternal life. We have come to believe and to know that you are the Holy One of God!" Jesus replied, "Didn't I choose you, the twelve, and yet one of you is the devil?" (Now he said this about Judas son of Simon Iscariot, for Judas, one of the twelve, was going to betray him.)

CHAPTER 7

THE FEAST OF SHELTERS

After this Jesus traveled throughout Galilee. He stayed out of Judea because the Jewish leaders wanted to kill him. Now the Jewish Feast of Shelters was near. So Jesus' brothers advised him, "Leave here and go to Judea so your disciples may see your miracles that you are performing. For no one who seeks to make a reputation for himself does anything in secret. If you are doing these things, show yourself to the world." (For not even his own brothers believed in him.)

So Jesus replied, "My time has not yet arrived, but you are ready at any opportunity! The world cannot hate you, but it hates me because I am testifying about it that its deeds are evil. You go up to the feast yourselves. I am not going up to this feast because my time has not yet fully arrived." When he had said this, he remained in Galilee.

But when his brothers had gone up to the feast, then Jesus himself also went up, not openly but in secret. So the Jewish leaders were looking for him at the feast, asking, "Where is he?" There was a lot of grumbling about him among the crowds. Some were saying, "He is a good man," but others, "He deceives the common people." However, no one spoke openly about him for fear of the Jewish leaders.

TEACHING IN THE TEMPLE

When the feast was half over, Jesus went up to the temple courts and began to teach. Then the Jewish leaders were astonished and said, "How does this man know so much when he has never had formal instruction?" So Jesus replied, "My teaching is not from me, but from the one who sent me. If anyone wants to do God's will, he will know about my teaching, whether it is from God or whether I speak from my own authority. The person who speaks on his own authority desires to receive honor for himself; the one who desires the honor of the one who sent him is a man of integrity, and there is no unrighteousness in him. Hasn't Moses given you the law? Yet not one of you keeps the law! Why do you want to kill me?"

The crowd answered, "You're possessed by a demon! Who is trying to kill you?" Jesus replied, "I performed one miracle and you are all amazed. However, because Moses gave you the practice of circumcision (not that it came from Moses, but from the forefathers), you circumcise a male child on the Sabbath. But if a male child is circumcised on the Sabbath so that the law of Moses is not broken, why are you angry with me because I made a man completely well on the Sabbath? Do not judge according to external appearance, but judge with proper judgment."

QUESTIONS ABOUT JESUS' IDENTITY

Then some of the residents of Jerusalem began to say, "Isn't this the man they are trying to kill? Yet here he is, speaking publicly, and they are saying nothing to him. Do the ruling authorities really know that this man is the Christ? But we know where this man comes from. Whenever the Christ comes, no one will know where he comes from."

Then Jesus, while teaching in the temple courts, cried out, "You both know me and know where I come from! And I have not come on my own initiative, but the one who sent me is true. You do not know him, but I know him because I have come from him and he sent me."

So then they tried to seize Jesus, but no one laid a hand on him because his time had not yet come. Yet many of the crowd believed in him and said, "Whenever the Christ comes, he won't perform more miraculous signs than this man did, will he?"

The Pharisees heard the crowd murmuring these things about Jesus, so the chief priests and the Pharisees sent officers to arrest him. Then Jesus said, "I will be with you for only a little while longer, and then I am going to the one who sent me. You will look for me but will not find me, and where I am you cannot come."

Then the Jewish leaders said to one another, "Where is he going to go that we cannot find him? He is not going to go to the Jewish people dispersed among the Greeks and teach the Greeks, is he? What did he mean by saying, 'You will look for me but will not find me, and where I am you cannot come'?"

TEACHING ABOUT THE SPIRIT

On the last day of the feast, the greatest day, Jesus stood up and shouted out, "If anyone is thirsty, let him come to me, and let the one who believes in me drink. Just as the scripture says, '***From within him will flow rivers of living water.***' " (Now he said this about the Spirit, whom those who believed in him were going to receive, for the Spirit had not yet been given because Jesus was not yet glorified.)

DIFFERING OPINIONS ABOUT JESUS

When they heard these words, some of the crowd began to say, "This really is the Prophet!" Others said, "This is the Christ!" But still others said, "No, for the Christ doesn't come from Galilee, does he? Don't the scriptures say that the Christ is *a descendant of David* and *comes from Bethlehem,* the village where David lived?" So there was a division in the crowd because of Jesus. Some of them were wanting to seize him, but no one laid a hand on him.

LACK OF BELIEF

Then the officers returned to the chief priests and Pharisees, who said to them, "Why didn't you bring him back with you?" The officers replied, "No one ever spoke like this man!" Then the Pharisees answered, "You haven't been deceived too, have you? None of the members of the ruling council or the Pharisees have believed in him, have they? But this rabble who do not know the law are accursed!"

Nicodemus, who had gone to Jesus before and who was one of the rulers, said, "Our law doesn't condemn a man unless it first hears from him and learns what he is doing, does it?" They replied, "You aren't from Galilee too, are you? Investigate carefully and you will see that no prophet comes from Galilee!"

A WOMAN CAUGHT IN ADULTERY

[[And each one departed to his own house.

CHAPTER 8

But Jesus went to the Mount of Olives. Early in the morning he came to the temple courts again. All the people came to him, and he sat down and began to teach them. The experts in the law and the Pharisees brought a woman who had been caught committing adultery. They made her stand in front of them and said to Jesus, "Teacher, this woman was caught in the very act of adultery. In the law *Moses commanded us to stone to death* such women. What then do you say?" (Now they were asking this in an attempt to trap him, so that they could bring charges against him.) Jesus bent down and wrote on the ground with his finger. When they persisted in asking him, he stood up straight and replied, "Whoever among you is guiltless may be the first to throw a stone at her." Then he bent over again and wrote on the ground.

Now when they heard this, they began to drift away one at a time, starting with the older ones, until Jesus was left alone with the woman standing before him. Jesus stood up straight and said to her, "Woman, where are they? Did no one condemn you?" She replied, "No one, Lord." And Jesus said, "I do not condemn you either. Go, and from now on do not sin any more."]]

JESUS AS THE LIGHT OF THE WORLD

Then Jesus spoke out again, "I am the light of the world! The one who follows me will never walk in darkness but will have the light of life." So the Pharisees objected, "You testify about yourself; your testimony is not true!" Jesus answered, "Even if I testify about myself, my testimony is true because I know where I came from and where I am going. But you people do not know where I came from or where I am going. You people judge by outward appearances; I do not judge anyone. But if I judge, my evaluation is accurate because I am not alone when I judge, but I and the Father who sent me do so together. It is written in your law that *the testimony of two men is true.* I testify about myself and the Father who sent me testifies about me."

Then they began asking him, "Who is your father?" Jesus answered, "You do not know either me or my Father. If you knew me you would know my Father too." (Jesus spoke these words near the offering box while he was teaching in the temple courts. No one seized him because his time had not yet come.)

WHERE JESUS CAME FROM AND WHERE HE IS GOING

Then Jesus said to them again, "I am going away, and you will look for me but will die in your sin. Where I am going you cannot come." So the Jewish leaders began to say, "Perhaps he is going to kill himself because he says, 'Where I am going you cannot come.' " Jesus replied, "You people are from below; I am from above. You people are from this world; I am not from this world. Thus I told you that you will die in your sins. For unless you believe that I am he, you will die in your sins."

So they said to him, "Who are you?" Jesus replied, "What I have told you from the beginning. I have many things to say and to judge about you, but the Father who sent me is truthful, and the things I have heard from him I speak to the world." (They did not understand that he was telling them about his Father.)

Then Jesus said, "When you lift up the Son of Man, then you will know that I am he, and I do nothing on my own initiative, but I speak just what the Father taught me. And the one who sent me is with me. He has not left me alone because I always do those things that please him." While he was saying these things, many people believed in him.

ABRAHAM'S CHILDREN AND THE DEVIL'S CHILDREN

Then Jesus said to those Judeans who had believed him, "If you continue to follow my teaching, you are really my disciples and you will know the truth, and the truth will set you free." "We are descendants of Abraham," they replied, "and have never been anyone's slaves! How can you say, 'You will become free'?" Jesus answered them, "I tell you the solemn truth, everyone who practices sin is a slave of sin. The slave does not remain in the family forever, but the son remains forever. So if the son sets you free, you will be really free. I know that you are Abraham's descendants. But you want to kill me because my teaching makes no progress among you. I am telling you the things I have seen while with the Father; as for you, practice the things you have heard from the Father!"

They answered him, "Abraham is our father!" Jesus replied, "If you are Abraham's children, you would be doing the deeds of Abraham. But now you are trying to kill me, a man who has told you the truth I heard from God. Abraham did not do this! You people are doing the deeds of your father."

Then they said to Jesus, "We were not born as a result of immorality! We have only one Father, God himself." Jesus replied, "If God were your Father, you would love me, for I have come from God and am now here. I have not come on my own initiative, but he sent me. Why don't you understand what I am saying? It is because you cannot accept my teaching. You people are from your father the devil, and you want to do what your father desires. He was a murderer from the beginning, and does not uphold the truth because there is no truth in him. Whenever he lies, he speaks according to his own nature because he is a liar and the father of lies. But because I am telling you the truth, you do not believe me. Who among you can prove me guilty of any sin? If I am telling you the truth, why don't you believe me? The one who belongs to God listens and responds to God's words. You don't listen and respond because you don't belong to God."

The Judeans replied, "Aren't we correct in saying that you are a Samaritan and are possessed by a demon?" Jesus answered, "I am not possessed by a demon, but I honor my

Father—and yet you dishonor me. I am not trying to get praise for myself. There is one who demands it, and he also judges. I tell you the solemn truth, if anyone obeys my teaching, he will never see death."

Then the Judeans responded, "Now we know you're possessed by a demon! Both Abraham and the prophets died, and yet you say, 'If anyone obeys my teaching, he will never experience death.' You aren't greater than our father Abraham who died, are you? And the prophets died too! Who do you claim to be?" Jesus replied, "If I glorify myself, my glory is worthless. The one who glorifies me is my Father, about whom you people say, 'He is our God.' Yet you do not know him, but I know him. If I were to say that I do not know him, I would be a liar like you. But I do know him, and I obey his teaching. Your father Abraham was overjoyed to see my day, and he saw it and was glad."

Then the Judeans replied, "You are not yet fifty years old! Have you seen Abraham?" Jesus said to them, "I tell you the solemn truth, before Abraham came into existence, I am!" Then they picked up stones to throw at him, but Jesus was hidden from them and went out from the temple area.

CHAPTER 9

HEALING A MAN BORN BLIND

Now as Jesus was passing by, he saw a man who had been blind from birth. His disciples asked him, "Rabbi, who committed the sin that caused him to be born blind, this man or his parents?" Jesus answered, "Neither this man nor his parents sinned, but he was born blind so that the acts of God may be revealed through what happens to him. We must perform the deeds of the one who sent me as long as it is daytime. Night is coming when no one can work. As long as I am in the world, I am the light of the world." Having said this, he spat on the ground and made some mud with the saliva. He smeared the mud on the blind man's eyes and said to him, "Go wash in the pool of Siloam" (which is translated "sent"). So the blind man went away and washed, and came back seeing.

Then the neighbors and the people who had seen him previously as a beggar began saying, "Is this not the man who used to sit and beg?" Some people said, "This is the man!" while others said, "No, but he looks like him." The man himself kept insisting, "I am the one!" So they asked him, "How then were you made to see?" He replied, "The man called Jesus made mud, smeared it on my eyes and told me, 'Go to Siloam and wash.' So I went and washed, and was able to see." They said to him, "Where is that man?" He replied, "I don't know."

THE PHARISEES' REACTION TO THE HEALING

They brought the man who used to be blind to the Pharisees. (Now the day on which Jesus made the mud and caused him to see was a Sabbath.) So the Pharisees asked him again how he had gained his sight. He replied, "He put mud on my eyes and I washed, and now I am able to see."

Then some of the Pharisees began to say, "This man is not from God because he does not observe the Sabbath." But others said, "How can a man who is a sinner perform such miraculous signs?" Thus there was a division among them. So again they asked the man who used to be blind, "What do you say about him, since he caused you to see?" "He is a prophet," the man replied.

Now the Jewish religious leaders refused to believe that he had really been blind and had gained his sight until at last they summoned the parents of the man who had become able to see. They asked the parents, "Is this your son, whom you say was born blind? Then how does he now see?" So his parents replied, "We know that this is our son and that he was born blind. But we do not know how he is now able to see, nor do we know who caused him to see. Ask him, he is a mature adult. He will speak for himself." (His parents said these things because they were afraid of the Jewish religious leaders. For the Jewish leaders had already agreed that anyone who confessed Jesus to be the Christ would be put out of the synagogue. For this reason his parents said, "He is a mature adult, ask him.")

Then they summoned the man who used to be blind a second time and said to him, "Promise before God to tell the truth. We know that this man is a sinner." He replied, "I do not know whether he is a sinner. I do know one thing—that although I was blind, now I can see." Then they said to him, "What did he do to you? How did he cause you to see?" He answered, "I told you already and you didn't listen. Why do you want to hear it again? You people don't want to become his disciples too, do you?"

They heaped insults on him, saying, "You are his disciple! We are disciples of Moses! We know that God has spoken to Moses! We do not know where this man comes from!" The man replied, "This is a remarkable thing that you don't know where he comes from, yet he caused me to see! We know that God doesn't listen to sinners, but if anyone is devout and does his will, God listens to him. Never before has anyone heard of someone causing a man born blind to see. If this man were not from God, he could do nothing." They replied, "You were born completely in sinfulness, and yet you presume to teach us?" So they threw him out.

THE MAN'S RESPONSE TO JESUS

Jesus heard that they had thrown him out, so he found the man and said to him, "Do you believe in the Son of Man?" The man replied, "And who is he, sir, that I may believe in him?" Jesus told him, "You have seen him; he is the one speaking with you." [He said, "Lord, I believe," and he worshiped him. Jesus said,] "For judgment I have come into this world, so that those who do not see may gain their sight, and the ones who see may become blind."

Some of the Pharisees who were with him heard this and asked him, "We are not blind too, are we?" Jesus replied, "If you were blind, you would not be guilty of sin, but now because you claim that you can see, your guilt remains.

CHAPTER 10

JESUS AS THE GOOD SHEPHERD

"I tell you the solemn truth, the one who does not enter the sheepfold by the door, but climbs in some other way, is a thief and a robber. The one who enters by the door is the shepherd of the sheep. The doorkeeper opens the door for him, and the sheep hear his voice. He calls his own sheep by name and leads them out. When he has brought all his own sheep out, he goes ahead of them, and the sheep follow him because they recognize his voice. They will never follow a stranger, but will run away from him because they do not recognize the stranger's voice." Jesus told them this parable, but they did not understand what he was saying to them.

So Jesus said again, "I tell you the solemn truth, I am the door for the sheep. All who came before me were thieves and robbers, but the sheep did not listen to them. I am the door. If anyone enters through me, he will be saved, and will come in and go out, and find pasture. The thief comes only to steal and kill and destroy; I have come so that they may have life, and may have it abundantly.

"I am the good shepherd. The good shepherd lays down his life for the sheep. The hired hand, who is not a shepherd and does not own sheep, sees the wolf coming and abandons the sheep and runs away. So the wolf attacks the sheep and scatters them. Because he is a hired hand and is not concerned about the sheep, he runs away.

"I am the good shepherd. I know my own and my own know me—just as the Father knows me and I know the Father—and I lay down my life for the sheep. I have other sheep that do not come from this sheepfold. I must bring them too, and they will listen to my voice, so that there will be one flock and one shepherd. This is why the Father loves me—because I lay down my life, so that I may take it back again. No one takes it away from me, but I lay it down of my own free will. I have the authority to lay it down, and I have the authority to take it back again. This commandment I received from my Father."

Another sharp division took place among the Jewish people because of these words. Many of them were saying, "He is possessed by a demon and has lost his mind! Why do you listen to him?" Others said, "These are not the words of someone possessed by a demon. A demon cannot cause the blind to see, can it?"

JESUS AT THE FEAST OF DEDICATION

Then came the feast of the Dedication in Jerusalem. It was winter, and Jesus was walking in the temple area in Solomon's Portico. The Jewish leaders surrounded him and asked, "How long will you keep us in suspense? If you are the Christ, tell us plainly." Jesus replied, "I told you and you do not believe. The deeds I do in my Father's name testify about me. But you refuse to believe because you are not my sheep. My sheep listen to my voice, and I know them, and they follow me. I give them eternal life, and they will never perish; no one will snatch them from my hand. My Father, who has given them to me, is greater than all, and no one can snatch them from my Father's hand. The Father and I are one."

The Jewish leaders picked up rocks again to stone him to death. Jesus said to them, "I have shown you many good deeds from the Father. For which one of them are you going to stone me?" The Jewish leaders replied, "We are not going to stone you for a good deed but for blasphemy because you, a man, are claiming to be God."

Jesus answered, "Is it not written in your law, '***I said, you are gods***'? If those people to whom the word of God came were called 'gods' (and the scripture cannot be broken), do you say about the one whom the Father set apart and sent into the world, 'You are blaspheming,' because I said, 'I am the Son of God'? If I do not perform the deeds of my Father, do not believe me. But if I do them, even if you do not believe me, believe the deeds, so that you may come to know and understand that I am in the Father and the Father is in me." Then they attempted again to seize him, but he escaped their clutches.

Jesus went back across the Jordan River again to the place where John had been baptizing at an earlier time, and he stayed there. Many came to him and began to say, "John performed no miraculous sign, but everything John said about this man was true!" And many believed in Jesus there.

CHAPTER 11

THE DEATH OF LAZARUS

Now a certain man named Lazarus was sick. He was from Bethany, the village where Mary and her sister Martha lived. (Now it was Mary who anointed the Lord with perfumed oil and wiped his feet dry with her hair, whose brother Lazarus was sick.) So the sisters sent a message to Jesus, "Lord, look, the one you love is sick." When Jesus heard this, he said, "This sickness will not lead to death, but to God's glory, so that the Son of God may be glorified through it." (Now Jesus loved Martha and her sister and Lazarus.)

So when he heard that Lazarus was sick, he remained in the place where he was for two more days. Then after this, he said to his disciples, "Let us go to Judea again." The disciples replied,

"Rabbi, the Jewish leaders were just now trying to stone you to death! Are you going there again?" Jesus replied, "Are there not 12 hours in a day? If anyone walks around in the daytime, he does not stumble because he sees the light of this world. But if anyone walks around at night, he stumbles because the light is not in him."

After he said this, he added, "Our friend Lazarus has fallen asleep. But I am going there to awaken him." Then the disciples replied, "Lord, if he has fallen asleep, he will recover." (Now Jesus had been talking about his death, but they thought he had been talking about real sleep.)

Then Jesus told them plainly, "Lazarus has died, and I am glad for your sake that I was not there, so that you may believe. But let us go to him." So Thomas (called Didymus) said to his fellow disciples, "Let us go too, so that we may die with him."

SPEAKING WITH MARTHA AND MARY

When Jesus arrived, he found that Lazarus had been in the tomb four days already. (Now Bethany was less than two miles from Jerusalem, so many of the Jewish people of the region had come to Martha and Mary to console them over the loss of their brother.) So when Martha heard that Jesus was coming, she went out to meet him, but Mary was sitting in the house. Martha said to Jesus, "Lord, if you had been here, my brother would not have died. But even now I know that whatever you ask from God, God will grant you."

Jesus replied, "Your brother will come back to life again." Martha said, "I know that he will come back to life again in the resurrection at the last day." Jesus said to her, "I am the resurrection and the life. The one who believes in me will live even if he dies, and the one who lives and believes in me will never die. Do you believe this?" She replied, "Yes, Lord, I believe that you are the Christ, the Son of God who comes into the world."

And when she had said this, Martha went and called her sister Mary, saying privately, "The Teacher is here and is asking for you." So when Mary heard this, she got up quickly and went to him. (Now Jesus had not yet entered the village, but was still in the place where Martha had come out to meet him.) Then the people who were with Mary in the house consoling her saw her get up quickly and go out. They followed her because they thought she was going to the tomb to weep there.

Now when Mary came to the place where Jesus was and saw him, she fell at his feet and said to him, "Lord, if you had been here, my brother would not have died." When Jesus saw her weeping, and the people who had come with her weeping, he was intensely moved in spirit and greatly distressed. He asked, "Where have you laid him?" They replied, "Lord, come and see." Jesus wept. Thus the people who had come to mourn said, "Look how much he loved him!" But some of them said, "This is the man who caused the blind man to see! Couldn't he have done something to keep Lazarus from dying?"

LAZARUS RAISED FROM THE DEAD

Jesus, intensely moved again, came to the tomb. (Now it was a cave, and a stone was placed across it.) Jesus said, "Take away the stone." Martha, the sister of the deceased, replied, "Lord, by this time the body will have a bad smell because he has been buried four days." Jesus responded, "Didn't I tell you that if you believe, you would see the glory of God?" So they took away the stone. Jesus looked upward and said, "Father, I thank you that you have listened to me. I knew that you always listen to me, but I said this for the sake of the crowd standing around here, that they may believe that you sent me." When he had said this, he shouted in a loud voice, "Lazarus, come out!" The one who had died came out, his feet and hands tied up with strips of cloth, and a cloth wrapped around his face. Jesus said to them, "Unwrap him and let him go."

THE RESPONSE OF THE JEWISH LEADERS

Then many of the people, who had come with Mary and had seen the things Jesus did, believed in him. But some of them went to the Pharisees and reported to them what Jesus had done. So the chief priests and the

Pharisees called the council together and said, "What are we doing? For this man is performing many miraculous signs. If we allow him to go on in this way, everyone will believe in him, and the Romans will come and take away our sanctuary and our nation."

Then one of them, Caiaphas, who was high priest that year, said, "You know nothing at all! You do not realize that it is more to your advantage to have one man die for the people than for the whole nation to perish." (Now he did not say this on his own, but because he was high priest that year, he prophesied that Jesus was going to die for the Jewish nation, and not for the Jewish nation only, but to gather together into one the children of God who are scattered.) So from that day they planned together to kill him.

Thus Jesus no longer went around publicly among the Judeans, but went away from there to the region near the wilderness, to a town called Ephraim, and stayed there with his disciples. Now the Jewish Feast of Passover was near, and many people went up to Jerusalem from the rural areas before the Passover to cleanse themselves ritually. Thus they were looking for Jesus, and saying to one another as they stood in the temple courts, "What do you think? That he won't come to the feast?" (Now the chief priests and the Pharisees had given orders that anyone who knew where Jesus was should report it, so that they could arrest him.)

CHAPTER 12

JESUS' ANOINTING

Then, six days before the Passover, Jesus came to Bethany, where Lazarus lived, whom he had raised from the dead. So they prepared a dinner for Jesus there. Martha was serving, and Lazarus was among those present at the table with him. Then Mary took three quarters of a pound of expensive aromatic oil from pure nard and anointed the feet of Jesus. She then wiped his feet dry with her hair. (Now the house was filled with the fragrance of the perfumed oil.) But Judas Iscariot, one of his disciples (the one who was going to betray him) said, "Why wasn't this oil sold for 300 silver coins and the money given to the poor?" (Now Judas said this not because he was concerned about the poor, but because he was a thief. As keeper of the money box, he used to steal what was put into it.) So Jesus said, "Leave her alone. She has kept it for the day of my burial. For you will always have the poor with you, but you will not always have me!"

Now a large crowd of Judeans learned that Jesus was there, and so they came not only because of him but also to see Lazarus whom he had raised from the dead. So the chief priests planned to kill Lazarus too, for on account of him many of the Jewish people from Jerusalem were going away and believing in Jesus.

THE TRIUMPHAL ENTRY

The next day the large crowd that had come to the feast heard that Jesus was coming to Jerusalem. So they took branches of palm trees and went out to meet him. They began to shout, ***"Hosanna! Blessed is the one who comes in the name of the Lord!*** Blessed is the king of Israel!" Jesus found a young donkey and sat on it, just as it is written, ***"Do not be afraid, people of Zion; look, your king is coming, seated on a donkey's colt!"*** (His disciples did not understand these things when they first happened, but when Jesus was glorified, then they remembered that these things were written about him and that these things had happened to him.)

So the crowd who had been with him when he called Lazarus out of the tomb and raised him from the dead were continuing to testify about it. Because they had heard that Jesus had performed this miraculous sign, the crowd went out to meet him. Thus the Pharisees said to one another, "You see that you can do nothing. Look, the world has run off after him!"

SEEKERS

Now some Greeks were among those who had gone up to worship at the feast. So these approached Philip, who was from Bethsaida in Galilee, and requested, "Sir, we would like to see Jesus." Philip went and told Andrew, and they both went and told Jesus. Jesus replied, "The time has come for the Son of Man to be glorified. I tell you the solemn truth, unless a kernel of wheat falls into the ground and dies, it remains by itself alone. But if it dies, it produces much grain. The one who loves his life destroys it, and the one who hates his life in this world guards it for eternal life. If anyone wants to serve me, he must follow me, and where I am, my servant will be too. If anyone serves me, the Father will honor him.

"Now my soul is greatly distressed. And what should I say? 'Father, deliver me from this hour'? No, but for this very reason I have come to this hour. Father, glorify your name." Then a voice came from heaven, "I have glorified it, and I will glorify it again." The crowd that stood there and heard the voice said that it had thundered. Others said that an angel had spoken to him. Jesus said, "This voice has not come for my benefit but for yours. Now is the judgment of this world; now the ruler of this world will be driven out. And I, when I am lifted up from the earth, will draw all people to myself." (Now he said this to indicate clearly what kind of death he was going to die.)

Then the crowd responded, "We have heard from the law that *the Christ will remain forever.* How can you say, 'The Son of Man must be lifted up'? Who is this Son of Man?" Jesus replied, "The light is with you for a little while longer. Walk while you have the light, so that the darkness may not overtake you. The one who walks in the darkness does not know where he is going. While you have the light, believe in the light, so that you may become sons of light." When Jesus had said these things, he went away and hid himself from them.

THE OUTCOME OF JESUS' PUBLIC MINISTRY FORETOLD

Although Jesus had performed so many miraculous signs before them, they still refused to believe in him, so that the word of the prophet Isaiah would be fulfilled. He said, ***"Lord, who has believed our message, and to whom has the arm of the Lord been revealed?"*** For this reason they could not believe because again Isaiah said,

> ***"He has blinded their eyes***
> ***and hardened their heart,***
> ***so that they would not see with their eyes***
> ***and understand with their heart,***
> ***and turn to me, and I would heal them."***

Isaiah said these things because he saw Christ's glory and spoke about him.

Nevertheless, even among the rulers many believed in him, but because of the Pharisees they would not confess Jesus to be the Christ, so that they would not be put out of the synagogue. For they loved praise from men more than praise from God.

JESUS' FINAL PUBLIC WORDS

But Jesus shouted out, "The one who believes in me does not believe in me, but in the one who sent me, and the one who sees me sees the one who sent me. I have come as a light into the world, so that everyone who believes in me should not remain in darkness. If anyone hears my words and does not obey them, I do not judge him. For I have not come to judge the world, but to save the world. The one who rejects me and does not accept my words has a judge; the word I have spoken will judge him at the last day. For I have not spoken from my own authority, but the Father himself who sent me has commanded me what I should say and what I should speak. And I know that his commandment is eternal life. Thus the things I say, I say just as the Father has told me."

CHAPTER 13

WASHING THE DISCIPLES' FEET

Just before the Passover Feast, Jesus knew that his time had come to depart from this world to the Father. Having loved his own who were in the world, he now loved them to the very end. The evening meal was in progress, and the devil had already put into the heart of Judas Iscariot, Simon's son, that he should betray Jesus. Because Jesus knew that the Father had handed all things over to him, and that he had come from God and was going back to God, he got up from the meal, removed his outer clothes, took a towel and tied it around himself. He poured water into the washbasin and began to wash the disciples' feet and to dry them with the towel he had wrapped around himself.

Then he came to Simon Peter. Peter said to him, "Lord, are you going to wash my feet?" Jesus replied, "You do not understand what I am doing now, but you will understand after these things." Peter said to him, "You will never wash my feet!" Jesus replied, "If I do not wash you, you have no share with me." Simon Peter said to him, "Lord, wash not only my feet but also my hands and my head!" Jesus replied, "The one who has bathed needs only to wash his feet, but is completely clean. And you disciples are clean, but not every one of you." (For Jesus knew the one who was going to betray him. For this reason he said, "Not every one of you is clean.")

So when Jesus had washed their feet and put his outer clothing back on, he took his place at the table again and said to them, "Do you understand what I have done for you? You call me 'Teacher' and 'Lord,' and do so correctly, for that is what I am. If I then, your Lord and Teacher, have washed your feet, you too ought to wash one another's feet. For I have given you an example—you should do just as I have done for you. I tell you the solemn truth, the slave is not greater than his master, nor is the one who is sent as a messenger greater than the one who sent him. If you understand these things, you will be blessed if you do them.

THE ANNOUNCEMENT OF JESUS' BETRAYAL

"What I am saying does not refer to all of you. I know the ones I have chosen. But this is to fulfill the scripture, '***The one who eats my bread has turned against me.***' I am telling you this now, before it happens, so that when it happens you may believe that I am he. I tell you the solemn truth, whoever accepts the one I send accepts me, and whoever accepts me accepts the one who sent me."

When he had said these things, Jesus was greatly distressed in spirit, and testified, "I tell you the solemn truth, one of you will betray me." The disciples began to look at one another, worried and perplexed to know which of them he was talking about. One of his disciples, the one Jesus loved, was at the table to the right of Jesus in a place of honor. So Simon Peter gestured to this disciple to ask Jesus who it was he was referring to. Then the disciple whom Jesus loved leaned back against Jesus' chest and asked him, "Lord, who is it?" Jesus replied, "It is the one to whom I will give this piece of bread after I have dipped it in the dish." Then he dipped the piece of bread in the dish and gave it to Judas Iscariot, Simon's son. And after Judas took the piece of bread, Satan entered into him. Jesus said to him, "What you are about to do, do quickly." (Now none of those present at the table understood why Jesus said this to Judas. Some thought that because Judas had the money box, Jesus was telling him to buy whatever they needed for the feast, or to give something to the poor.) Judas took the piece of bread and went out immediately. (Now it was night.)

THE PREDICTION OF PETER'S DENIAL

When Judas had gone out, Jesus said, "Now the Son of Man is glorified, and God is glorified in him. If God is glorified in him, God will also glorify him in himself, and he will glorify him right away. Children, I am still with you for a little while. You will look for me, and just as I said to the Jewish religious leaders, 'Where I am going you cannot come,' now I tell you the same.

"I give you a new commandment–to love one another. Just as I have loved you, you also are to love one another. Everyone will know by this that you are my disciples–if you have love for one another."

Simon Peter said to him, "Lord, where are you going?" Jesus replied, "Where I am going, you cannot follow me now, but you will follow later." Peter said to him, "Lord, why can't I follow you now? I will lay down my life for you!" Jesus answered, "Will you lay down your life for me? I tell you the solemn truth, the rooster will not crow until you have denied me three times!

CHAPTER 14

JESUS' PARTING WORDS TO HIS DISCIPLES

"Do not let your hearts be distressed. You believe in God; believe also in me. There are many dwelling places in my Father's house. Otherwise, I would have told you, because I am going away to make ready a place for you. And if I go and make ready a place for you, I will come again and take you to be with me, so that where I am you may be too. And you know the way where I am going."

Thomas said, "Lord, we don't know where you are going. How can we know the way?" Jesus replied, "I am the way, and the truth, and the life. No one comes to the Father except through me. If you have known me, you will know my Father too. And from now on you do know him and have seen him."

Philip said, "Lord, show us the Father, and we will be content." Jesus replied, "Have I been with you for so long and yet you have not known me, Philip? The person who has seen me has seen the Father! How can you say, 'Show us the Father'? Do you not believe that I am in the Father, and the Father is in me? The words that I say to you, I do not speak on my own initiative, but the Father residing in me performs his miraculous deeds. Believe me that I am in the Father, and the Father is in me, but if you do not believe me, believe because of the miraculous deeds themselves. I tell you the solemn truth, the person who believes in me will perform the miraculous deeds that I am doing, and will perform greater deeds than these because I am going to the Father. And I will do whatever you ask in my name, so that the Father may be glorified in the Son. If you ask me anything in my name, I will do it.

TEACHING ON THE HOLY SPIRIT

"If you love me, you will obey my commandments. Then I will ask the Father, and he will give you another Advocate to be with you forever—the Spirit of truth, whom the world cannot accept because it does not see him or know him. But you know him because he resides with you and will be in you.

"I will not abandon you as orphans, I will come to you. In a little while the world will not see me any longer, but you will see me; because I live, you will live too. You will know at that time that I am in my Father and you are in me and I am in you. The person who has my commandments and obeys them is the one who loves me. The one who loves me will be loved by my Father, and I will love him and will reveal myself to him."

"Lord," Judas (not Judas Iscariot) said, "what has happened that you are going to reveal yourself to us and not to the world?" Jesus replied, "If anyone loves me, he will obey my word, and my Father will love him, and we will come to him and take up residence with him. The person who does not love me does not obey my words. And the word you hear is not mine, but the Father's who sent me.

"I have spoken these things while staying with you. But the Advocate, the Holy Spirit, whom the Father will send in my name, will teach you everything and will cause you to remember everything I said to you.

"Peace I leave with you; my peace I give to you; I do not give it to you as the world does. Do not let your hearts be distressed or lacking in courage. You heard me say to you, 'I am going away and I am coming back to you.' If you loved me, you would be glad that I am going to the Father because the Father is greater than I am. I have told you now before it happens, so that when it happens you may believe. I will not speak with you much longer, for the ruler of this world is coming. He has no power over me, but I am doing just what the Father commanded me, so that the world may know that I love the Father. Get up, let us go from here.

CHAPTER 15

THE VINE AND THE BRANCHES

"I am the true vine and my Father is the gardener. He takes away every branch that does not bear fruit in me. He prunes every branch that bears fruit so that it will bear more fruit. You are clean already because of the word that I have spoken to you. Remain in me, and I will remain in you. Just as the branch cannot bear fruit by itself, unless it remains in the vine, so neither can you unless you remain in me.

"I am the vine; you are the branches. The one who remains in me—and I in him—bears much fruit because apart from me you can accomplish nothing. If anyone does not remain in me, he is thrown out like a branch and dries up; and such branches are gathered up and thrown into the fire and are burned up. If you remain in me and my words remain in you, ask whatever you want, and it will be done for you. My Father is honored by this, that you bear much fruit and show that you are my disciples.

"Just as the Father has loved me, I have also loved you; remain in my love. If you obey my commandments, you will remain in my love, just as I have obeyed my Father's commandments and remain in his love. I have told you these things so that my joy may be in you, and your joy may be complete. My commandment is this—to love one another just as I have loved you. No one has greater love than this—that one lays down his life for his friends. You are my friends if you do what I command you. I no longer call you slaves because the slave does not understand what his master is doing. But I have called you friends because I have revealed to you everything I heard from my Father. You did not choose me, but I chose you and appointed you to go and bear fruit, fruit that remains, so that whatever you ask the Father in my name he will give you. This I command you—to love one another.

THE WORLD'S HATRED

"If the world hates you, be aware that it hated me first. If you belonged to the world, the world would love you as its own. However, because you do not belong to the world, but I chose you out of the world, for this reason the world hates you. Remember what I told you, 'A slave is not greater than his master.' If they persecuted me, they will also persecute you. If they obeyed my word, they will obey yours too. But they will do all these things to you on account of my name because they do not know the one who sent me. If I had not come and spoken to them, they would not be guilty of sin. But they no longer have any excuse for their sin. The one who hates me hates my Father too. If I had not performed among them the miraculous deeds that no one else did, they would not be guilty of sin. But now they have seen the deeds and have hated both me and my Father. Now this happened to fulfill the word that is written in their law, '***They hated me without reason.***' When the Advocate comes, whom I will send you from the Father—the Spirit of truth who goes out from the Father—he will testify about me, and you also will testify because you have been with me from the beginning.

CHAPTER 16

"I have told you all these things so that you will not fall away. They will put you out of the synagogue, yet a time is coming when the one who kills you will think he is offering service to God. They will do these things because they have not known the Father or me. But I have told you these things so that when their time comes, you will remember that I told you about them.

"I did not tell you these things from the beginning because I was with you. But now I am going to the one who sent me, and not one of you is asking me, 'Where are you going?' Instead your hearts are filled with sadness because I have said these things to you. But I tell you the truth, it is to your advantage that I am going away. For if I do not go away, the Advocate will not come to you, but if I go, I will send him to you. And when he comes, he will prove the world wrong concerning sin and righteousness and judgment—concerning sin because they do not believe in me; concerning righteousness because I am going to the Father and you will see me no longer; and concerning judgment because the ruler of this world has been condemned.

"I have many more things to say to you, but you cannot bear them now. But when he, the Spirit of truth, comes, he will guide you into all truth. For he will not speak on his own authority, but will speak whatever he hears and will tell you what is to come. He will glorify me because he will receive from me what is mine and will tell it to you. Everything that the Father has is mine; that is why I said the Spirit will receive from me what is mine and will tell it to you. In a little while you will see me no longer; again after a little while, you will see me."

Then some of his disciples said to one another, "What is the meaning of what he is saying, 'In a little while you will not see me; again after a little while, you will see me,' and 'because I am going to the Father'?" So they kept on repeating, "What is the meaning of what he says, 'In a little while'? We do not understand what he is talking about."

Jesus could see that they wanted to ask him about these things, so he said to them, "Are you asking each other about this—that I said, 'In a little while you will not see me; again after a little while, you will see me'? I tell you the solemn truth, you will weep and wail, but the world will rejoice; you will be sad, but your sadness will turn into joy. When a woman gives birth, she has distress because her time has come, but when her child is born, she no longer remembers the suffering because of her joy that a human being has been born into the world. So also you have sorrow now, but *I will see you again, and your hearts will rejoice, and no one will take your joy away from you.* At that time you will ask me nothing. I tell you the solemn truth, whatever you ask the Father in my name he will give you. Until now you have not asked for anything in my name. Ask and you will receive it, so that your joy may be complete.

"I have told you these things in obscure figures of speech; a time is coming when I will no longer speak to you in obscure figures, but will tell you plainly about the Father. At that time you will ask in my name, and I do not say that I will ask the Father on your behalf. For the Father himself loves you because you have loved me and have believed that I came from God. I came from the Father and entered into the world, but in turn, I am leaving the world and going back to the Father."

His disciples said, "Look, now you are speaking plainly and not in obscure figures of speech! Now we know that you know everything and do not need anyone to ask you anything. Because of this we believe that you have come from God."

Jesus replied, "Do you now believe? Look, a time is coming—and has come—when you will be scattered, each one to his own home, and I will be left alone. Yet I am not alone because my Father is with me. I have told you these things so that in me you may have peace. In the world you have trouble and suffering, but take courage—I have conquered the world."

CHAPTER 17

JESUS PRAYS FOR THE FATHER TO GLORIFY HIM

When Jesus had finished saying these things, he looked upward to heaven and said, "Father, the time has come. Glorify your Son, so that your Son may glorify you—just as you have given him authority over all humanity, so that he may give eternal life to everyone you have given him. Now this is eternal life—that they know you, the only true God, and Jesus Christ, whom you sent. I glorified you on earth by completing the work you gave me to do. And now,

Father, glorify me at your side with the glory I had with you before the world was created.

JESUS PRAYS FOR THE DISCIPLES

"I have revealed your name to the men you gave me out of the world. They belonged to you, and you gave them to me, and they have obeyed your word. Now they understand that everything you have given me comes from you, because I have given them the words you have given me. They accepted them and really understand that I came from you, and they believed that you sent me. I am praying on behalf of them. I am not praying on behalf of the world, but on behalf of those you have given me because they belong to you. Everything I have belongs to you, and everything you have belongs to me, and I have been glorified by them. I am no longer in the world, but they are in the world, and I am coming to you. Holy Father, keep them safe in your name that you have given me, so that they may be one just as we are one. When I was with them I kept them safe and watched over them in your name that you have given me. Not one of them was lost except the one destined for destruction, so that the scripture could be fulfilled. But now I am coming to you, and I am saying these things in the world, so they may experience my joy completed in themselves. I have given them your word, and the world has hated them because they do not belong to the world, just as I do not belong to the world. I am not asking you to take them out of the world, but that you keep them safe from the evil one. They do not belong to the world just as I do not belong to the world. Set them apart in the truth; your word is truth. Just as you sent me into the world, so I sent them into the world. And I set myself apart on their behalf, so that they too may be truly set apart.

JESUS PRAYS FOR BELIEVERS EVERYWHERE

"I am not praying only on their behalf, but also on behalf of those who believe in me through their testimony, that they will all be one, just as you, Father, are in me and I am in you. I pray that they will be in us, so that the world will believe that you sent me. The glory you gave to me I have given to them, that they may be one just as we are one—I in them and you in me—that they may be completely one, so that the world will know that you sent me, and you have loved them just as you have loved me.

"Father, I want those you have given me to be with me where I am, so that they can see my glory that you gave me because you loved me before the creation of the world. Righteous Father, even if the world does not know you, I know you, and these men know that you sent me. I made known your name to them, and I will continue to make it known, so that the love you have loved me with may be in them, and I may be in them."

CHAPTER 18

BETRAYAL AND ARREST

When he had said these things, Jesus went out with his disciples across the Kidron Valley. There was an orchard there, and he and his disciples went into it. (Now Judas, the one who betrayed him, knew the place too, because Jesus had met there many times with his disciples.) So Judas obtained a squad of soldiers and some officers of the chief priests and Pharisees. They came to the orchard with lanterns and torches and weapons.

Then Jesus, because he knew everything that was going to happen to him, came and asked them, "Who are you looking for?" They replied, "Jesus the Nazarene." He told them, "I am he." (Now Judas, the one who betrayed him, was standing there with them.) So when Jesus said to them, "I am he," they retreated and fell to the ground. Then Jesus asked them again, "Who are you looking for?" And they said, "Jesus the Nazarene." Jesus replied, "I told you that I am he. If you are looking for me, let these men go." He said this to fulfill the word he had spoken, "I have not lost a single one of those whom you gave me."

Then Simon Peter, who had a sword, pulled it out and struck the high priest's slave, cutting off his right ear. (Now the slave's name was Malchus.) But Jesus said to Peter, "Put your sword back into its sheath! Am I not to drink the cup that the Father has given me?"

JESUS BEFORE ANNAS

Then the squad of soldiers with their commanding officer and the officers of the Jewish leaders arrested Jesus and tied him up. They brought him first to Annas, for he was the father-in-law of Caiaphas, who was high priest that year. (Now it was Caiaphas who had advised the Jewish leaders that it was to their advantage that one man die for the people.)

PETER'S FIRST DENIAL

Simon Peter and another disciple followed them as they brought Jesus to Annas. (Now the other disciple was acquainted with the high priest, and he went with Jesus into the high priest's courtyard.) But Peter was left standing outside by the door. So the other disciple who was acquainted with the high priest came out and spoke to the slave girl who watched the door, and brought Peter inside. The girl who was the doorkeeper said to Peter, "You're not one of this man's disciples too, are you?" He replied, "I am not." (Now the slaves and the guards were standing around a charcoal fire they had made, warming themselves because it was cold. Peter also was standing with them, warming himself.)

JESUS QUESTIONED BY ANNAS

While this was happening, the high priest questioned Jesus about his disciples and about his teaching. Jesus replied, "I have spoken publicly to the world. I always taught in the synagogues and in the temple courts, where all the Jewish people assemble together. I have said nothing in secret. Why do you ask me? Ask those who heard what I said. They know what I said." When Jesus had said this, one of the high priest's officers who stood nearby struck him on the face and said, "Is that the way you answer the high priest?" Jesus replied, "If I have said something wrong, confirm what is wrong. But if I spoke correctly, why strike me?" Then Annas sent him, still tied up, to Caiaphas the high priest.

PETER'S SECOND AND THIRD DENIALS

Meanwhile Simon Peter was standing in the courtyard warming himself. They said to him, "You aren't one of his disciples too, are you?" Peter denied it: "I am not!" One of the high priest's slaves, a relative of the man whose ear Peter had cut off, said, "Did I not see you in the orchard with him?" Then Peter denied it again, and immediately a rooster crowed.

JESUS BROUGHT BEFORE PILATE

Then they brought Jesus from Caiaphas to the Roman governor's residence. (Now it was very early morning.) They did not go into the governor's residence so they would not be ceremonially defiled, but could eat the Passover meal. So Pilate came outside to them and said, "What accusation do you bring against this man?" They replied, "If this man were not a criminal, we would not have handed him over to you."

Pilate told them, "Take him yourselves and pass judgment on him according to your own law!" The Jewish leaders replied, "We cannot legally put anyone to death." (This happened to fulfill the word Jesus had spoken when he indicated what kind of death he was going to die.)

PILATE QUESTIONS JESUS

So Pilate went back into the governor's residence, summoned Jesus, and asked him, "Are you the king of the Jews?" Jesus replied, "Are you saying this on your own initiative, or have others told you about me?" Pilate answered, "I am not a Jew, am I? Your own people and your chief priests handed you over to me. What have you done?"

Jesus replied, "My kingdom is not from this world. If my kingdom were from this world, my servants would be fighting to keep me from being handed over to the Jewish authorities. But as it is, my kingdom is not from here." Then Pilate said, "So you are a king!" Jesus replied, "You say that I am a king. For this reason I was born, and for this reason I came into the world—to testify to the truth. Everyone who belongs to the truth listens to my voice." Pilate asked, "What is truth?"

When he had said this he went back outside to the Jewish leaders and announced, "I find no basis for an accusation against him. But it is your custom that I release one prisoner for you at the Passover. So do you want me to release for you the king of the Jews?" Then they shouted back, "Not this man, but Barabbas!" (Now Barabbas was a revolutionary.)

CHAPTER 19

PILATE TRIES TO RELEASE JESUS

Then Pilate took Jesus and had him flogged severely. The soldiers braided a crown of thorns and put it on his head, and they clothed him in a purple robe. They came up to him again and again and said, "Hail, king of the Jews!" And they struck him repeatedly in the face.

Again Pilate went out and said to the Jewish leaders, "Look, I am bringing him out to you, so that you may know that I find no reason for an accusation against him." So Jesus came outside, wearing the crown of thorns and the purple robe. Pilate said to them, "Look, here is the man!" When the chief priests and their officers saw him, they shouted out, "Crucify him! Crucify him!" Pilate said, "You take him and crucify him! Certainly I find no reason for an accusation against him!" The Jewish leaders replied, "We have a law, and according to our law he ought to die because he claimed to be the Son of God!"

When Pilate heard what they said, he was more afraid than ever, and he went back into the governor's residence and said to Jesus, "Where do you come from?" But Jesus gave him no answer. So Pilate said, "Do you refuse to speak to me? Don't you know I have the authority to release you and to crucify you?" Jesus replied, "You would have no authority over me at all, unless it was given to you from above. Therefore the one who handed me over to you is guilty of greater sin."

From this point on, Pilate tried to release him. But the Jewish leaders shouted out, "If you release this man, you are no friend of Caesar! Everyone who claims to be a king opposes Caesar!" When Pilate heard these words he brought Jesus outside and sat down on the judgment seat in the place called "The Stone Pavement" (*Gabbatha* in Aramaic). (Now it was the day of preparation for the Passover, about noon.) Pilate said to the Jewish leaders, "Look, here is your king!"

Then they shouted out, "Away with him! Away with him! Crucify him!" Pilate asked, "Shall I crucify your king?" The high priests replied, "We have no king except Caesar!" Then Pilate handed him over to them to be crucified.

THE CRUCIFIXION

So they took Jesus, and carrying his own cross he went out to the place called "The Place of the Skull" (called in Aramaic *Golgotha*). There they crucified him along with two others, one on each side, with Jesus in the middle. Pilate also had a notice written and fastened to the cross, which read: "Jesus the Nazarene, the king of the Jews." Thus many of the Jewish residents of Jerusalem read this notice because the place where Jesus was crucified was near the city, and the notice was written in Aramaic, Latin, and Greek. Then the chief priests of the Jews said to Pilate, "Do not write, 'The king of the Jews,' but rather, 'This man said, I am king of the Jews.'" Pilate answered, "What I have written, I have written."

Now when the soldiers crucified Jesus, they took his clothes and made four shares, one for each soldier, and the tunic remained. (Now the tunic was seamless, woven from top to bottom as a single piece.) So the soldiers said to one another, "Let's not tear it, but throw dice to see who will get it." This took place to fulfill the scripture that says, "***They divided my garments among them, and for my clothing they threw dice.***" So the soldiers did these things.

Now standing beside Jesus' cross were his mother, his mother's sister, Mary the wife of Clopas, and Mary Magdalene. So when Jesus saw his mother and the disciple whom he loved standing there, he said to his mother, "Woman, look, here is your son!" He then said to his disciple, "Look, here is your mother!" From that very time the disciple took her into his own home.

JESUS' DEATH

After this Jesus, realizing that by this time everything was completed, said (in order to fulfill the scripture), "I am thirsty!" A jar full of sour wine was there, so they put a sponge soaked in sour wine on a branch of hyssop and lifted it to his mouth. When he had received the sour wine, Jesus said, "It is completed!" Then he bowed his head and gave up his spirit.

Then because it was the day of preparation, so that the bodies should not stay on the crosses on the Sabbath (for that Sabbath was an especially important one), the Jewish leaders asked Pilate to have the victims' legs broken and the bodies taken down. So the soldiers came and broke the legs of the two men who had been crucified with Jesus, first the one and then the other. But when they came to Jesus and saw that he was already dead, they did not break his legs. But one of the soldiers pierced his side with a spear, and blood and water flowed out immediately. And the person who saw it has testified (and his testimony is true, and he knows that he is telling the truth), so that you also may believe. For these things happened so that the scripture would be fulfilled, ***"Not a bone of his will be broken."*** And again another scripture says, ***"They will look on the one whom they have pierced."***

JESUS' BURIAL

After this, Joseph of Arimathea, a disciple of Jesus (but secretly because he feared the Jewish leaders), asked Pilate if he could remove the body of Jesus. Pilate gave him permission, so he went and took the body away. Nicodemus, the man who had previously come to

Jesus at night, accompanied Joseph, carrying a mixture of myrrh and aloes weighing about 75 pounds. Then they took Jesus' body and wrapped it, with the aromatic spices, in strips of linen cloth according to Jewish burial customs. Now at the place where Jesus was crucified there was a garden, and in the garden was a new tomb where no one had yet been buried. And so, because it was the Jewish day of preparation and the tomb was nearby, they placed Jesus' body there.

CHAPTER 20

THE RESURRECTION

Now very early on the first day of the week, while it was still dark, Mary Magdalene came to the tomb and saw that the stone had been moved away from the entrance. So she went running to Simon Peter and the other disciple whom Jesus loved and told them, "They have taken the Lord from the tomb, and we don't know where they have put him!" Then Peter and the other disciple set out to go to the tomb. The two were running together, but the other disciple ran faster than Peter and reached the tomb first. He bent down and saw the strips of linen cloth lying there, but he did not go in. Then Simon Peter, who had been following him, arrived and went right into the tomb. He saw the strips of linen cloth lying there, and the face cloth, which had been around Jesus' head, not lying with the strips of linen cloth but rolled up in a place by itself. Then the other disciple, who had reached the tomb first, came in, and he saw and believed. (For they did not yet understand the scripture that Jesus must rise from the dead.)

JESUS' APPEARANCE TO MARY MAGDALENE

So the disciples went back to their homes. But Mary stood outside the tomb weeping. As she wept, she bent down and looked into the tomb. And she saw two angels in white sitting where Jesus' body had been lying, one at the head and one at the feet. They said to her, "Woman, why are you weeping?" Mary replied, "They have taken my Lord away, and I do not know where they have put him!" When she had said this, she turned around and saw Jesus standing there, but she did not know that it was Jesus.

Jesus said to her, "Woman, why are you weeping? Who are you looking for?" Because she thought he was the gardener, she said to him, "Sir, if you have carried him away, tell me where you have put him, and I will take him." Jesus said to her, "Mary." She turned and said to him in Aramaic, "*Rabboni*" (which means "Teacher"). Jesus replied, "Do not touch me, for I have not yet ascended to my Father. Go to my brothers and tell them, 'I am ascending to my Father and your Father, to my God and your God.' " Mary Magdalene came and informed the disciples, "I have seen the Lord!" And she told them what Jesus had said to her.

JESUS' APPEARANCE TO THE DISCIPLES

On the evening of that day, the first day of the week, the disciples had gathered together and locked the doors of the place because they were afraid of the Jewish leaders. Jesus came and stood among them and said to them, "Peace be with you." When he had said this, he showed them his hands and his side. Then the disciples rejoiced when they saw the Lord. So Jesus said to them again, "Peace be with you. Just as the Father has sent me, I also send you." And after he said this, he breathed on them and said, "Receive the Holy Spirit. If you forgive anyone's sins, they are forgiven; if you retain anyone's sins, they are retained."

THE RESPONSE OF THOMAS

Now Thomas (called Didymus), one of the twelve, was not with them when Jesus came. The other disciples told him, "We have seen the Lord!" But he replied, "Unless I see the wounds from the nails in his hands, and put my finger into the wounds from the nails, and put my hand into his side, I will never believe it!"

Eight days later the disciples were again together in the house, and Thomas was with them. Although the doors were locked, Jesus came and stood among them and said, "Peace be with you!" Then he said to Thomas, "Put your finger here, and examine my hands. Extend your hand and put it into my side. Do not continue in your unbelief, but believe."

Thomas replied to him, "My Lord and my God!" Jesus said to him, "Have you believed because you have seen me? Blessed are the people who have not seen and yet have believed."

Now Jesus performed many other miraculous signs in the presence of the disciples, which are not recorded in this book. But these are recorded so that you may believe that Jesus is the Christ, the Son of God, and that by believing you may have life in his name.

CHAPTER 21

JESUS' APPEARANCE TO THE DISCIPLES IN GALILEE

After this Jesus revealed himself again to the disciples by the Sea of Tiberias. Now this is how he did so. Simon Peter, Thomas (called Didymus), Nathanael (who was from Cana in Galilee), the sons of Zebedee, and two other disciples of his were together. Simon Peter told them, "I am going fishing." "We will go with you," they replied. They went out and got into the boat, but that night they caught nothing.

When it was already very early morning, Jesus stood on the beach, but the disciples did not know that it was Jesus. So Jesus said to them, "Children, you don't have any fish, do you?" They replied, "No." He told them, "Throw your net on the right side of the boat, and you will find some." So they threw the net and were not able to pull it in because of the large number of fish.

Then the disciple whom Jesus loved said to Peter, "It is the Lord!" So Simon Peter, when he heard that it was the Lord, tucked in his outer garment (for he had nothing on underneath it), and plunged into the sea. Meanwhile the other disciples came with the boat, dragging the net full of fish, for they were not far from land, only about a hundred yards.

When they got out on the beach, they saw a charcoal fire ready with a fish placed on it, and bread. Jesus said, "Bring some of the fish you have just now caught." So Simon Peter went aboard and pulled the net to shore. It was full of large fish, 153, but although there were so many, the net was not torn. "Come, have breakfast," Jesus said. But none of the disciples dared to ask him, "Who are you?" because they knew it was the Lord. Jesus came and took the bread and gave it to them, and did the same with the fish. This was now the third time Jesus was revealed to the disciples after he was raised from the dead.

PETER'S RESTORATION

Then when they had finished breakfast, Jesus said to Simon Peter, "Simon, son of John, do you love me more than these do?" He replied, "Yes, Lord, you know I love you." Jesus told him, "Feed my lambs." Jesus said a second time, "Simon, son of John, do you love me?" He replied, "Yes, Lord, you know I love you." Jesus told him, "Shepherd my sheep." Jesus said a third time, "Simon, son of John, do you love me?" Peter was distressed that Jesus asked him a third time, "Do you love me?" and said, "Lord, you know everything. You know that I love you." Jesus replied, "Feed my sheep. I tell you the solemn truth, when you were young, you tied your clothes around you and went wherever you wanted, but when you are old, you will stretch out your hands, and others will tie you up and bring you where you do not want to go." (Now Jesus said this to indicate clearly by what kind of death Peter was going to glorify God.) After he said this, Jesus told Peter, "Follow me."

PETER AND THE DISCIPLE JESUS LOVED

Peter turned around and saw the disciple whom Jesus loved following them. (This was the disciple who had leaned back against Jesus' chest at the meal and asked, "Lord, who is the one who is going to betray you?") So when Peter saw him, he asked Jesus, "Lord, what about him?" Jesus replied, "If I want him to live until I come back, what concern is that of yours? You follow me!" So the saying circulated among the brothers and sisters that this disciple was not going to die. But Jesus did not say to him that he was not going to die, but rather, "If I want him to live until I come back, what concern is that of yours?"

A FINAL NOTE

This is the disciple who testifies about these things and has written these things, and we know that his testimony is true. There are many other things that Jesus did. If every one of them were written down, I suppose the whole world would not have room for the books that would be written.

1 JOHN

PROLOGUE

For over sixty years John had faithfully served Jesus. They had traveled together along Israel's dusty roads between villages where Jesus proclaimed salvation found only in him. John had been one of the few followers present at the pivotal yet painful moment of Jesus' crucifixion. After Jesus' resurrection and ascension, John continued fulfilling the assignment Jesus had given him, sharing the gospel in both speech and writing.

John was now in the sunset of his life, but it was no time to set aside his mission. Word had reached him that false teachers known as the Gnostics were causing doubt and confusion in the church. These teachers claimed that Jesus had given a "secret" knowledge to certain people, and only those who had this knowledge—the Gnostics themselves—were saved.

With a mixture of authority and sensitivity, John wrote to end the uncertainty. There was no secret knowledge. Salvation was found not in covert whisperings of Jesus, but rather in what he had done and cried out in the open. There was a way that people could know they were saved, and John was going to make that way clear.

CHAPTER 1

THE PROLOGUE TO THE LETTER

This is what we proclaim to you: what was from the beginning, what we have heard, what we have seen with our eyes, what we have looked at and our hands have touched (concerning the word of life—and the life was revealed, and we have seen and testify and announce to you the eternal life that was with the Father and was revealed to us). What we have seen and heard we announce to you too, so that you may have fellowship with us (and indeed our fellowship is with the Father and with his Son Jesus Christ). Thus we are writing these things so that our joy may be complete.

GOD IS LIGHT, SO WE MUST WALK IN THE LIGHT

Now this is the gospel message we have heard from him and announce to you: God is light, and in him there is no darkness at all. If we say we have fellowship with him and yet keep on walking in the darkness, we are lying and not practicing the truth. But if we walk in the light as he himself is in the light, we have fellowship with one another and the blood of Jesus his Son cleanses us from all sin. If we say we do not bear the guilt of sin, we are deceiving ourselves and the truth is not in us. But if we confess our sins, he is faithful and righteous, forgiving us our sins and cleansing us from all unrighteousness. If we say we have not sinned, we make him a liar and his word is not in us.

CHAPTER 2

(My little children, I am writing these things to you so that you may not sin.) But if anyone does sin, we have an advocate with the Father, Jesus Christ the Righteous One, and he himself is the atoning sacrifice for our sins, and not only for our sins but also for the whole world.

KEEPING GOD'S COMMANDMENTS

Now by this we know that we have come to know God: if we keep his commandments. The one who says "I have come to know God" and yet does not keep his commandments is a liar, and the truth is not in such a person. But whoever obeys his word, truly in this person the love of God has been perfected. By this we know that we are in him. The one who says he resides in God ought himself to walk just as Jesus walked.

Dear friends, I am not writing a new commandment to you, but an old commandment which you have had from the beginning. The old commandment is the word that you have already heard. On the other hand, I am writing a new commandment to you, which is true in him and in you, because the darkness is passing away and the true light is already shining. The one who says he is in the light but still hates his fellow Christian is still in the darkness. The one who loves his fellow Christian resides in the light, and there is no cause for stumbling in him. But the one who hates his fellow Christian is in the darkness, walks in the darkness, and does not know where he is going because the darkness has blinded his eyes.

WORDS OF REASSURANCE

I am writing to you, little children, that your sins have been forgiven because of his name. I am writing to you, fathers, that you have known him who has been from the beginning. I am writing to you, young people, that you have conquered the evil one. I have written to you, children, that you have known the Father. I have written to you, fathers, that you have known him who has been from the beginning. I have written to you, young people, that you are strong, and the word of God resides in you, and you have conquered the evil one.

Do not love the world or the things in the world. If anyone loves the world, the love of the Father is not in him, because all that is in the world (the desire of the flesh and the desire of the eyes and the arrogance produced by material possessions) is not from the Father, but is from the world. And the world is passing away with all its desires, but the person who does the will of God remains forever.

WARNING ABOUT FALSE TEACHERS

Children, it is the last hour, and just as you heard that the antichrist is coming, so now many antichrists have appeared. We know from this that it is the last hour. They went out from us, but they did not really belong to us because if they had belonged to us, they would have remained with us. But they went out from us to demonstrate that all of them do not belong to us.

Nevertheless you have an anointing from the Holy One, and you all know. I have not written to you that you do not know the truth, but that you do know it, and that no lie is of the truth. Who is the liar but the person who denies that Jesus is the Christ? This one is the antichrist: the person who denies the Father and the Son. Everyone who denies the Son does not have the Father either. The person who confesses the Son has the Father also.

As for you, what you have heard from the beginning must remain in you. If what you heard from the beginning remains in you, you also will remain in the Son and in the

Father. Now this is the promise that he himself made to us: eternal life. These things I have written to you about those who are trying to deceive you.

Now as for you, the anointing that you received from him resides in you, and you have no need for anyone to teach you. But as his anointing teaches you about all things, it is true and is not a lie. Just as it has taught you, you reside in him.

CHILDREN OF GOD

And now, little children, remain in him, so that when he appears we may have confidence and not shrink away from him in shame when he comes back. If you know that he is righteous, you also know that everyone who practices righteousness has been fathered by him.

CHAPTER 3

(See what sort of love the Father has given to us: that we should be called God's children—and indeed we are! For this reason the world does not know us: Because it did not know him. Dear friends, we are God's children now, and what we will be has not yet been revealed. We know that whenever it is revealed we will be like him because we will see him just as he is. And everyone who has this hope focused on him purifies himself, just as Jesus is pure).

Everyone who practices sin also practices lawlessness; indeed, sin is lawlessness. And you know that Jesus was revealed to take away sins, and in him there is no sin. Everyone who resides in him does not sin; everyone who sins has neither seen him nor known him. Little children, let no one deceive you: The one who practices righteousness is righteous, just as Jesus is righteous. The one who practices sin is of the devil because the devil has been sinning from the beginning. For this purpose the Son of God was revealed: to destroy the works of the devil. Everyone who has been fathered by God does not practice sin because God's seed resides in him, and thus he is not able to sin because he has been fathered by God. By this the children of God and the children of the devil are revealed: Everyone who does not practice righteousness—the one who does not love his fellow Christian—is not of God.

GOD IS LOVE, SO WE MUST LOVE ONE ANOTHER

For this is the gospel message that you have heard from the beginning: that we should love one another, not like Cain who was of the evil one and brutally murdered his brother. And why did he murder him? Because his deeds were evil, but his brother's were righteous.

Therefore do not be surprised, brothers and sisters, if the world hates you. We know that we have crossed over from death to life because we love our fellow Christians. The one who does not love remains in death. Everyone who hates his fellow Christian is a murderer, and you know that no murderer has eternal life residing in him. We have come to know love by this: that Jesus laid down his life for us; thus we ought to lay down our lives for our fellow Christians. But whoever has the world's possessions and sees his fellow Christian in need and shuts off his compassion against him, how can the love of God reside in such a person?

Little children, let us not love with word or with tongue but in deed and truth. And by this we will know that we are of the truth and will convince our conscience in his presence, that if our conscience condemns us, that God is greater than our conscience and knows all things. Dear friends, if our conscience does not condemn us, we have confidence in the presence of God, and whatever we ask we receive from him, because we keep his commandments and do the things that are pleasing to him. Now this is his commandment: that we believe in the name of his Son Jesus Christ and love one another, just as he gave us the commandment. And the person who keeps his commandments resides in God, and God in him. Now by this we know that God resides in us: by the Spirit he has given us.

CHAPTER 4

TESTING THE SPIRITS

Dear friends, do not believe every spirit, but test the spirits to determine if they are from God, because many false prophets have gone out into the world. By this you know the Spirit of God: Every spirit that confesses Jesus as the Christ who has come in the flesh is from God, but every spirit that refuses to confess Jesus, that spirit is not from God, and this is the spirit of the antichrist, which you have heard is coming, and now is already in the world.

You are from God, little children, and have conquered them because the one who is in you is greater than the one who is in the world. They are from the world; therefore they speak from the world's perspective and the world listens to them. We are from God; the person who knows God listens to us, but whoever is not from God does not listen to us. By this we know the Spirit of truth and the spirit of deceit.

GOD IS LOVE

Dear friends, let us love one another, because love is from God, and everyone who loves has been fathered by God and knows God. The person who does not love does not know God because God is love. By this the love of God is revealed in us: that God has sent his one and only Son into the world so that we may live through him. In this is love: not that we have loved God, but that he loved us and sent his Son to be the atoning sacrifice for our sins.

Dear friends, if God so loved us, then we also ought to love one another. No one has seen God at any time. If we love one another, God resides in us, and his love is perfected in us. By this we know that we reside in God and he in us: in that he has given us of his Spirit. And we have seen and testify that the Father has sent the Son to be the Savior of the world.

If anyone confesses that Jesus is the Son of God, God resides in him and he in God. And we have come to know and to believe the love that God has in us. God is love, and the one who resides in love resides in God, and God resides in him. By this love is perfected with us, so that we may have confidence in the day of judgment, because just as Jesus is, so also are we in this world. There is no fear in love, but perfect love drives out fear because fear has to do with punishment. The one who fears punishment has not been perfected in love. We love because he loved us first.

If anyone says "I love God" and yet hates his fellow Christian, he is a liar because the one who does not love his fellow Christian whom he has seen cannot love God whom he has not seen. And the commandment we have from him is this: that the one who loves God should love his fellow Christian too.

CHAPTER 5

Everyone who believes that Jesus is the Christ has been fathered by God, and everyone who loves the father loves the child fathered by him. By this we know that we love the children of God: whenever we love God and obey his commandments. For this is the love of God: that we keep his commandments. And his commandments do not weigh us down, because everyone who has been fathered by God conquers the world.

TESTIMONY ABOUT THE SON

This is the conquering power that has conquered the world: our faith. Now who is the person who has conquered the world except the one who believes that Jesus is the Son of God? Jesus Christ is the one who came by water and blood—not by the water only, but by the water and the blood. And the Spirit is the one who testifies, because the Spirit is the truth. For there are three that testify, the Spirit and the water and the blood, and these three are in agreement.

If we accept the testimony of men, the testimony of God is greater because this is the testimony of God that he has testified concerning his Son. (The one who believes in the Son of God has the testimony in himself; the one who does not believe God has made him a liar because he has not believed in the testimony that God has testified concerning his

Son.) And this is the testimony: God has given us eternal life, and this life is in his Son. The one who has the Son has this eternal life; the one who does not have the Son of God does not have this eternal life.

ASSURANCE OF ETERNAL LIFE

I have written these things to you who believe in the name of the Son of God so that you may know that you have eternal life.

And this is the confidence that we have before him: that whenever we ask anything according to his will, he hears us. And if we know that he hears us in regard to whatever we ask, then we know that we have the requests that we have asked from him. If anyone sees his fellow Christian committing a sin not resulting in death, he should ask, and God will grant life to the person who commits a sin not resulting in death. There is a sin resulting in death. I do not say that he should ask about that. All unrighteousness is sin, but there is sin not resulting in death.

We know that everyone fathered by God does not sin, but God protects the one he has fathered, and the evil one cannot touch him. We know that we are from God, and the whole world lies in the power of the evil one. And we know that the Son of God has come and has given us insight to know him who is true, and we are in him who is true, in his Son Jesus Christ. This one is the true God and eternal life. Little children, guard yourselves from idols.

2 JOHN

PROLOGUE

False teachers continued to plague the church. Once again, John knew he had to speak up and address this serious problem. He needed to remind the church that it could not let its guard down. The church could not grow weary of shielding itself. But John also knew that living in such a prolonged defensive posture could lead to another mistake, one just as dangerous. John would have to warn against this threat as well.

CHAPTER 1

INTRODUCTION AND THANKSGIVING

From the elder, to an elect lady and her children, whom I love in truth (and not I alone, but also all those who know the truth), because of the truth that resides in us and will be with us forever. Grace, mercy, and peace will be with us from God the Father and from Jesus Christ the Son of the Father, in truth and love.

I rejoiced greatly because I have found some of your children living according to the truth, just as the Father commanded us.

WARNING AGAINST FALSE TEACHERS

But now I ask you, lady (not as if I were writing a new commandment to you, but the one we have had from the beginning), that we love one another. (Now this is love: that we walk according to his commandments.) This is the commandment, just as you have heard from the beginning; thus you should walk in it. For many deceivers have gone out into the world, people who do not confess Jesus as Christ coming in the flesh. This person is the deceiver and the antichrist! Watch out, so that you do not lose the things we have worked for, but receive a full reward.

Everyone who goes on ahead and does not remain in the teaching of Christ does not have God. The one who remains in this teaching has both the Father and the Son. If anyone comes to you and does not bring this teaching, do not receive him into your house and do not give him any greeting because the person who gives him a greeting shares in his evil deeds.

CONCLUSION

Though I have many other things to write to you, I do not want to do so with paper and ink, but I hope to come visit you and speak face to face so that our joy may be complete.

The children of your elect sister greet you.

3 JOHN

PROLOGUE

In John's first two epistles, he had dealt with false teachers, guiding the church on how best to deal with them. Now, however, John wanted to be sure that the church remembered the opposite as well. False teachers were always to be rejected, but fellow believers were always to be accepted. Providing lodging and a meal for a believer might not seem important, but John wanted the church to know the difference such hospitality makes.

CHAPTER 1

INTRODUCTION AND THANKSGIVING

From the elder, to Gaius my dear brother, whom I love in truth. Dear friend, I pray that all may go well with you and that you may be in good health, just as it is well with your soul. For I rejoiced greatly when the brothers came and testified to your truth, just as you are living according to the truth.

I have no greater joy than this: to hear that my children are living according to the truth.

THE CHARGE TO GAIUS

Dear friend, you demonstrate faithfulness by whatever you do for the brothers (even though they are strangers). They have testified to your love before the church. You will do well to send them on their way in a manner worthy of God. For they have gone forth on behalf of "The Name," accepting nothing from the pagans. Therefore we ought to support such people so that we become coworkers in cooperation with the truth.

DIOTREPHES THE TROUBLEMAKER

I wrote something to the church, but Diotrephes, who loves to be first among them, does not acknowledge us. Therefore, if I come, I will call attention to the deeds he is doing—the bringing of unjustified charges against us with evil words! And not being content with that, he not only refuses to welcome the brothers himself, but hinders the people who want to do so and throws them out of the church! Dear friend, do not imitate what is bad, but what is good. The one who does good is of God; the one who does what is bad has not seen God.

WORTHY DEMETRIUS

Demetrius has been testified to by all, even by the truth itself. We also testify to him, and you know that our testimony is true.

CONCLUSION

I have many things to write to you, but I do not wish to write to you with pen and ink. But I hope to see you right away, and we will speak face to face. Peace be with you. The friends here greet you. Greet the friends there by name.

REVELATION

PROLOGUE

John probably didn't imagine that seeing his friend would happen this way. More than sixty years had passed since John last set eyes on Jesus. As his final days slipped by, John found himself a prisoner exiled on the Island of Patmos. He thought often of the reunion that was drawing close. But then one day John had a most startling vision. He saw Jesus. But John didn't see his friend the way he remembered him. He saw him in a way he never expected.

Jesus told John that he was to write down everything he was about to experience, including what he was seeing now. It was not an easy assignment. How can you put into words creatures and events that no eye has ever seen? How do you describe sounds that no ear has ever heard? As John struggled to find the right words and right images to convey his experience, there were times when even he seemed to be confused by it all. If what he saw was challenging to him, how could he expect those who read his depiction to understand? His task was considerable, but it was worth it. He was given a vision about the end of history, everything we know, and the beginning of everything being made new.

John knew that what the church most needed to know was not found in any of the details, as important as they might be. The key to the entire vision he had been given was found in the one who had given it to him: Jesus.

CHAPTER 1

THE PROLOGUE

The revelation of Jesus Christ, which God gave him to show his servants what must happen very soon. He made it clear by sending his angel to his servant John, who then testified to everything that he saw concerning the word of God and the testimony about Jesus Christ. Blessed is the one who reads the words of this prophecy aloud, and blessed are those who hear and obey the things written in it, because the time is near!

From John, to the seven churches that are in the province of Asia: Grace and peace to you from "he who is," and who was, and who is still to come, and from the seven spirits who are before his throne, and from Jesus Christ—the faithful witness, the firstborn from among the dead, the ruler over the kings of the earth. To the one who loves us and has set us free from our sins at the cost of his own blood and has appointed us as a kingdom, as priests serving his God and Father—to him be the glory and the power for ever and ever! Amen.

> (Look! *He is returning with the clouds,*
> and *every eye will see him,*
> *even those who pierced him,*
> and all the tribes on the earth will
> mourn because of him.
> This will certainly come to pass! Amen.)

"I am the Alpha and the Omega," says the Lord God—the one who is, and who was, and who is still to come—the All-Powerful!

I, John, your brother and the one who shares with you in the persecution, kingdom, and endurance that are in Jesus, was on the island called Patmos because of the word of God and the testimony about Jesus. I was in the Spirit on the Lord's Day when I heard behind me a loud voice like a trumpet, saying: "Write in a book what you see and send it to the seven churches—to Ephesus, Smyrna, Pergamum, Thyatira, Sardis, Philadelphia, and Laodicea."

I turned to see whose voice was speaking to me, and when I did so, I saw seven golden lampstands, and in the midst of the lampstands was one *like a son of man.* He was dressed in a robe extending down to his feet, and he wore a wide golden belt around his chest. His head and hair were as white as wool, even as white as snow, and his eyes were like a fiery flame. His feet were like polished bronze refined in a furnace, and his voice was like the roar of many waters. He held seven stars in his right hand, and a sharp double-edged sword extended out of his mouth. His face shone like the sun shining at full strength. When I saw him I fell down at his feet as though I were dead, but he placed his right hand on me and said: "Do not be afraid! I am the first and the last, and the one who lives! I was dead, but look, now I am alive—forever and ever—and I hold the keys of death and of Hades! Therefore write what you saw, what is, and what will be after these things. The mystery of the seven stars that you saw in my right hand and the seven golden lampstands is this: The seven stars are the angels of the seven churches, and the seven lampstands are the seven churches.

CHAPTER 2

TO THE CHURCH IN EPHESUS

"To the angel of the church in Ephesus, write the following:

"This is the solemn pronouncement of the one who has a firm grasp on the seven stars in his right hand—the one who walks among the seven golden lampstands: 'I know your works as well as your labor and steadfast endurance, and that you cannot tolerate evil. You have even put to the test those who refer to themselves as apostles (but are not), and have discovered that they are false. I am also aware that you have persisted steadfastly, endured much for the sake of my name, and have not grown weary. But I have this against you: You have departed from your first love! Therefore, remember from what high state you have fallen and repent! Do the deeds you did at the first; if not, I will come to you and remove your lampstand from its place—that is, if you do not repent. But you do have this going for you: You hate what the Nicolaitans practice—practices I also hate. The one who has an ear had better hear what the Spirit says to the churches. To the one who conquers, I will permit him to eat from the tree of life that is in the paradise of God.'

TO THE CHURCH IN SMYRNA

"To the angel of the church in Smyrna write the following:

"This is the solemn pronouncement of the one who is the first and the last, the one who was dead, but came to life: 'I know the distress you are suffering and your poverty (but you are rich). I also know the slander against you by those who call themselves Jews and really are not, but are a synagogue of Satan. Do not be afraid of the things you are about to suffer. The devil is about to have some of you thrown into prison so you may be tested, and you will experience suffering for ten days. Remain faithful even to the point of death, and I will give you the crown that is life itself. The one who has an ear had better hear what the Spirit says to the churches. The one who conquers will in no way be harmed by the second death.'

TO THE CHURCH IN PERGAMUM

"To the angel of the church in Pergamum write the following:

"This is the solemn pronouncement of the one who has the sharp double-edged sword: 'I know where you live—where Satan's throne is. Yet you continue to cling to my name, and you have not denied your faith in me, even in the days of Antipas, my faithful witness, who was killed in your city where Satan lives. But I have a few things against you: You have some people there who follow the teaching of Balaam, who instructed Balak to put a stumbling block before the people of Israel so they would eat food sacrificed to idols and commit sexual immorality. In the same way, there are also some among you who follow the teaching of the Nicolaitans. Therefore, repent! If not, I will come against you quickly and make war against those people with the sword of my mouth. The one who has an ear had better hear what the Spirit says to the churches. To the one who conquers, I will give him some of the hidden manna, and I will give him a white stone, and on that stone will be written a new name that no one can understand except the one who receives it.'

TO THE CHURCH IN THYATIRA

"To the angel of the church in Thyatira write the following:

"This is the solemn pronouncement of the Son of God, the one who has eyes like a fiery flame and whose feet are like polished bronze: 'I know your deeds: your love, faith, service, and steadfast endurance. In fact, your more recent deeds are greater than your earlier ones. But I have this against you: You tolerate that woman Jezebel, who calls herself a prophetess, and by her teaching deceives my servants to commit sexual immorality and to eat food sacrificed to idols. I have given her time to repent, but she is not willing to repent of her sexual immorality. Look! I am throwing her onto a bed of violent illness, and those who commit adultery with her into terrible suffering, unless they repent of her deeds. Furthermore, I will strike her followers with a deadly disease, and then all the churches will know that I am the one who searches minds and hearts. I will repay each one of you what your deeds deserve. But to the rest of you in Thyatira, all who do not hold to this teaching (who have not learned the so-called "deep secrets of Satan"), to you I say: I do not put any additional burden on you. However, hold on to what you have until I come. And to the one who conquers and who continues in my deeds until the end, I will give him authority over the nations—

he will rule them with an iron rod,
and like clay jars he will break them to
pieces,

just as I have received the right to rule from my Father—and I will give him the morning star. The one who has an ear had better hear what the Spirit says to the churches.'

CHAPTER 3

TO THE CHURCH IN SARDIS

"To the angel of the church in Sardis write the following:

"This is the solemn pronouncement of the one who holds the seven spirits of God and the seven stars: 'I know your deeds, that you have a reputation that you are alive, but in reality you are dead. Wake up then, and strengthen what remains that was about to die, because I have not found your deeds complete in the sight of my God. Therefore, remember what you received and heard, and obey it, and repent. If you do not wake up, I will come like a thief, and you will never know at what hour I will come against you. But you have a few individuals in Sardis who have not stained their clothes, and they will walk with me dressed in white because they are worthy. The one who conquers will be dressed like them in white clothing, and I will never erase his name from the book of life, but will declare his name before my Father and before his angels. The one who has an ear had better hear what the Spirit says to the churches.'

TO THE CHURCH IN PHILADELPHIA

"To the angel of the church in Philadelphia write the following:

"This is the solemn pronouncement of the Holy One, the True One, who holds the key of David, who opens doors no one can shut, and shuts doors no one can open: 'I know your deeds. (Look! I have put in front of you an open door that no one can shut.) I know that you have little strength, but you have obeyed my word and have not denied my name. Listen! I am going to make those people from the synagogue of Satan—who say they are Jews yet are not, but are lying—look, I will make them come and bow down at your feet and acknowledge that I have loved you. Because you have kept my admonition to endure steadfastly, I will also keep you from the hour of testing that is about to come on the whole world to test those who live on the earth. I am coming soon. Hold on to what you have so that no one can take away your crown. The one who conquers I will make a pillar in the temple of my God, and he will never depart from it. I will write on him the name of my God and the name of the city of my God (the new Jerusalem that comes down out of heaven from my God), and my new name as well. The one who has an ear had better hear what the Spirit says to the churches.'

TO THE CHURCH IN LAODICEA

"To the angel of the church in Laodicea write the following:

"This is the solemn pronouncement of the Amen, the faithful and true witness, the originator of God's creation: 'I know your deeds, that you are neither cold nor hot. I wish you were either cold or hot! So because you are lukewarm, and neither hot nor cold, I am going to vomit you out of my mouth! Because you say, "I am rich and have acquired great wealth, and need nothing," but do not realize that you are wretched, pitiful, poor, blind, and naked, take my advice and buy gold from me refined by fire so you can become rich! Buy from me white clothing so you can be clothed and your shameful nakedness will not be exposed, and buy eye salve to put on your eyes so you can see! All those I love, I rebuke and discipline. So be earnest and repent! Listen! I am standing at the door and knocking! If anyone hears my voice and opens the door I will come into his home and share a meal with him, and he with me. I will grant the one who conquers permission to sit with me on my throne, just as I, too, conquered and sat down with my Father on his throne. The one who has an ear had better hear what the Spirit says to the churches.' "

CHAPTER 4

THE AMAZING SCENE IN HEAVEN

After these things I looked, and there was a door standing open in heaven! And the first voice I had heard speaking to me like a trumpet said: "Come up here so that I can show you what must happen after these things." Immediately I was in the Spirit, and a throne was standing in heaven with someone seated on it! And the one seated on it was like jasper and carnelian in appearance, and a rainbow looking like it was made of emerald encircled the throne. In a circle around the throne were twenty-four other thrones, and seated on those thrones were twenty-four elders. They were dressed in white clothing and had golden crowns on their heads. From the throne came out flashes of lightning and roaring and crashes of thunder. Seven flaming torches, which are the seven spirits of God, were burning in front of the throne, and in front of the throne was something like a sea of glass, like crystal.

In the middle of the throne and around the throne were four living creatures full of eyes in front and in back. The first living creature was like a lion, the second creature like an ox, the third creature had a face like a man's, and the fourth creature looked like an eagle flying. Each one of the four living creatures had six wings and was full of eyes all around and inside. They never rest day or night, saying:

"***Holy, Holy, Holy is the Lord God, the All-Powerful,***
Who was, and who is, and who is still to come!"

And whenever the living creatures give glory, honor, and thanks to the one who sits on the throne, who lives forever and ever, the twenty-four elders throw themselves to the ground before the one who sits on the throne and worship the one who lives forever and ever, and they offer their crowns before his throne, saying:

"You are worthy, our Lord and God,
to receive glory and honor and power,
since you created all things,
and because of your will they existed and were created!"

CHAPTER 5

THE OPENING OF THE SCROLL

Then I saw in the right hand of the one who was seated on the throne a scroll written on the front and back and sealed with seven seals. And I saw a powerful angel proclaiming in a loud voice: "Who is worthy to open the scroll and to break its seals?" But no one in heaven or on earth or under the earth was able to open the scroll or look into it. So I began weeping bitterly because no one was found who was worthy to open the scroll or to look into it. Then one of the elders said to me, "Stop weeping! Look, the Lion of the tribe of Judah, the root of David, has conquered; thus he can open the scroll and its seven seals."

Then I saw standing in the middle of the throne and of the four living creatures, and in the middle of the elders, a Lamb that appeared to have been killed. He had seven horns and seven eyes, which are the seven spirits of God sent out into all the earth. Then he came and took the scroll from the right hand of the one who was seated on the throne, and when he had taken the scroll, the four living creatures and the twenty-four elders threw themselves to the ground before the Lamb. Each of them had a harp and golden bowls full of incense (which are the prayers of the saints). They were singing a new song:

"You are worthy to take the scroll
and to open its seals
because you were killed,
and at the cost of your own blood you
have purchased for God
persons from every tribe, language,
people, and nation.
You have appointed them as a kingdom
and priests to serve our God, and they
will reign on the earth."

Then I looked and heard the voice of many angels in a circle around the throne, as well as the living creatures and the elders.

Their number was ten thousand times ten thousand—thousands times thousands—all of whom were singing in a loud voice:

"Worthy is the lamb who was killed
to receive power and wealth
and wisdom and might
and honor and glory and praise!"

Then I heard every creature—in heaven, on earth, under the earth, in the sea, and all that is in them—singing:

"To the one seated on the throne and to the Lamb
be praise, honor, glory, and ruling power forever and ever!"

And the four living creatures were saying "Amen," and the elders threw themselves to the ground and worshiped.

CHAPTER 6

THE SEVEN SEALS

I looked on when the Lamb opened one of the seven seals, and I heard one of the four living creatures saying with a thunderous voice, "Come!" So I looked, and here came a white horse! The one who rode it had a bow, and he was given a crown, and as a conqueror he rode out to conquer.

Then when the Lamb opened the second seal, I heard the second living creature saying, "Come!" And another horse, fiery red, came out, and the one who rode it was granted permission to take peace from the earth so that people would butcher one another, and he was given a huge sword.

Then when the Lamb opened the third seal I heard the third living creature saying, "Come!" So I looked, and here came a black horse! The one who rode it had a balance scale in his hand. Then I heard something like a voice from among the four living creatures saying, "A quart of wheat will cost a day's pay, and three quarts of barley will cost a day's pay. But do not damage the olive oil and the wine!"

Then when the Lamb opened the fourth seal I heard the voice of the fourth living creature saying, "Come!" So I looked and here came a pale green horse! The name of the one who rode it was Death, and Hades followed right behind. They were given authority over a fourth of the earth, to kill its population with the sword, famine, and disease, and by the wild animals of the earth.

Now when the Lamb opened the fifth seal, I saw under the altar the souls of those who had been violently killed because of the word of God and because of the testimony they had given. They cried out with a loud voice, "How long, Sovereign Master, holy and true, before you judge those who live on the earth and avenge our blood?" Each of them was given a long white robe, and they were told to rest for a little longer, until the full number was reached of both their fellow servants and their brothers who were going to be killed just as they had been.

Then I looked when the Lamb opened the sixth seal, and a huge earthquake took place; the sun became as black as sackcloth made of hair, and the full moon became blood red; and the stars in the sky fell to the earth like a fig tree dropping its unripe figs when shaken by a fierce wind. The sky was split apart like a scroll being rolled up, and every mountain and island was moved from its place. Then the kings of the earth, the very important people, the generals, the rich, the powerful, and everyone, slave and free, hid themselves in the caves and among the rocks of the mountains. They said to the mountains and to the rocks, "Fall on us and hide us from the face of the one who is seated on the throne and from the wrath of the Lamb, because the great day of their wrath has come, and who is able to withstand it?"

CHAPTER 7

THE SEALING OF THE 144,000

After this I saw four angels standing at the four corners of the earth, holding back the four winds of the earth so no wind could blow on the earth, on the sea, or on any tree. Then I saw another angel ascending from the east, who had the seal of the living God. He shouted out with a loud voice to the four angels who had been given permission to damage the earth and the sea: "Do not damage the earth or the sea or the trees until we have put a seal on the foreheads of the servants of our God." Now I heard the number of those who were marked with the seal, 144,000, sealed from all the tribes of the people of Israel:

From the tribe of Judah, 12,000 were sealed,
from the tribe of Reuben, 12,000,
from the tribe of Gad, 12,000,
from the tribe of Asher, 12,000,
from the tribe of Naphtali, 12,000,
from the tribe of Manasseh, 12,000,
from the tribe of Simeon, 12,000,
from the tribe of Levi, 12,000,
from the tribe of Issachar, 12,000,
from the tribe of Zebulun, 12,000,
from the tribe of Joseph, 12,000,
from the tribe of Benjamin, 12,000 were sealed.

After these things I looked, and here was an enormous crowd that no one could count, made up of persons from every nation, tribe, people, and language, standing before the throne and before the Lamb dressed in long white robes, and with palm branches in their hands. They were shouting out in a loud voice,

"Salvation belongs to our God, who is seated on the throne, and to the Lamb!"

And all the angels stood there in a circle around the throne and around the elders and the four living creatures, and they threw themselves down with their faces to the ground before the throne and worshiped God, saying,

"Amen! Praise and glory,
and wisdom and thanksgiving,
and honor and power and strength
be to our God for ever and ever. Amen!"

Then one of the elders asked me, "These dressed in long white robes—who are they and where have they come from?" So I said to him, "My lord, you know the answer." Then he said to me, "These are the ones who have come out of the great tribulation. They have washed their robes and made them white in the blood of the Lamb! For this reason they are before the throne of God, and they serve him day and night in his temple, and the one seated on the throne will shelter them. *They will never go hungry or be thirsty again, and the sun will not beat down on them, nor any burning heat,* because the Lamb in the middle of the throne will shepherd them and lead them to springs of living water, *and God will wipe away every tear from their eyes.*"

CHAPTER 8

THE SEVENTH SEAL

Now when the Lamb opened the seventh seal there was silence in heaven for about half an hour. Then I saw the seven angels who stand before God, and seven trumpets were given to them. Another angel holding a golden censer came and was stationed at the altar. A large amount of incense was given to him to offer up, with the prayers of all the saints, on the golden altar that is before the throne. The smoke coming from the incense, along with the prayers of the saints, ascended before God from the angel's hand. Then the angel took the censer, filled it with fire from the altar, and threw it on the earth, and there were crashes of thunder, roaring, flashes of lightning, and an earthquake.

Now the seven angels holding the seven trumpets prepared to blow them.

The first angel blew his trumpet, and there was hail and fire mixed with blood, and it was thrown at the earth so that a third of the earth was burned up, a third of the trees were burned up, and all the green grass was burned up.

Then the second angel blew his trumpet, and something like a great mountain of burning fire was thrown into the sea. A third of the sea became blood, and a third of the creatures living in the sea died, and a third of the ships were completely destroyed.

Then the third angel blew his trumpet, and a huge star burning like a torch fell from the sky; it landed on a third of the rivers and on the springs of water. (Now the name of the star is Wormwood.) So a third of the waters became wormwood, and many people died from these waters because they were poisoned.

Then the fourth angel blew his trumpet, and a third of the sun was struck, and a third of the moon, and a third of the stars, so that a third of them were darkened. And there was no light for a third of the day and for a third of the night likewise. Then I looked, and I heard an eagle flying directly overhead, proclaiming with a loud voice, "Woe! Woe! Woe to those who live on the earth because of the remaining sounds of the trumpets of the three angels who are about to blow them!"

CHAPTER 9

Then the fifth angel blew his trumpet, and I saw a star that had fallen from the sky to the earth, and he was given the key to the shaft of the abyss. He opened the shaft of the abyss and smoke rose out of it like smoke from a giant furnace. The sun and the air were darkened with smoke from the shaft. Then out of the smoke came locusts onto the earth, and they were given power like that of the scorpions of the earth. They were told not to damage the grass of the earth, or any green plant or tree, but only those people who did not have the seal of God on their forehead. The locusts were not given permission to kill them, but only to torture them for five months, and their torture was like that of a scorpion when it stings a person. In those days people will seek death, but will not be able to find it; they will long to die, but death will flee from them.

Now the locusts looked like horses equipped for battle. On their heads were something like crowns similar to gold, and their faces looked like men's faces. They had hair like women's hair, and their teeth were like lions' teeth. They had breastplates like iron breastplates, and the sound of their wings was like the noise of many horse-drawn chariots charging into battle. They have tails and stingers like scorpions, and their ability to injure people for five months is in their tails. They have as king over them the angel of the abyss, whose name in Hebrew is *Abaddon,* and in Greek, *Apollyon.*

The first woe has passed, but two woes are still coming after these things!

Then the sixth angel blew his trumpet, and I heard a single voice coming from the horns on the golden altar that is before God, saying to the sixth angel, the one holding the trumpet, "Set free the four angels who are bound at the great river Euphrates!" Then the four angels who had been prepared for this hour, day, month, and year were set free to kill a third of humanity. The number of soldiers on horseback was 200,000,000; I heard their number. Now this is what the horses and their riders looked like in my vision: The riders had breastplates that were fiery red, dark blue, and sulfurous yellow in color. The heads of the horses looked like lions' heads, and fire, smoke, and sulfur came out of their mouths. A third of humanity was killed by these three plagues, that is, by the fire, the smoke, and the sulfur that came out of their mouths. For the power of the horses resides in their mouths and in their tails because their tails are like snakes, having heads that inflict injuries. The rest of humanity, who had not been killed by these plagues, did not repent of the works of their hands so that they did not stop worshiping demons and idols made of gold, silver, bronze, stone, and wood—idols that cannot see or hear or walk about. Furthermore, they did not repent of their murders, of their magic spells, of their sexual immorality, or of their stealing.

CHAPTER 10

THE ANGEL WITH THE LITTLE SCROLL

Then I saw another powerful angel descending from heaven, wrapped in a cloud, with a rainbow above his head; his face was like the sun, and his legs were like pillars of fire. He held in his hand a little scroll that was open, and he put his right foot on the sea and his left on the land. Then he shouted in a loud voice like a lion roaring, and when he shouted, the seven thunders sounded their voices. When the seven thunders spoke, I was preparing to write, but just then I heard a voice from heaven say, "Seal up what the seven thunders spoke and do not write it down." Then the angel I saw standing on the sea and on the land raised his right hand to heaven and swore by the one who lives forever and ever, who created heaven and what is in it, and the earth and what is in it, and the sea and what is in it, "There will be no more delay! But in the days when the seventh angel is about to blow his trumpet, the mystery of God is completed, just as he has proclaimed to his servants the prophets." Then the voice I had heard from heaven began to speak to me again, "Go and take the open scroll in the hand of the angel who is standing on the sea and on the land." So I went to the angel and asked him to give me the little scroll. He said to me, "Take the scroll and eat it. It will make your stomach bitter, but it will be as sweet as honey in your mouth." So I took the little scroll from the angel's hand and ate it, and it did taste as sweet as honey in my mouth, but when I had eaten it, my stomach became bitter. Then they told me: "You must prophesy again about many peoples, nations, languages, and kings."

CHAPTER 11

THE FATE OF THE TWO WITNESSES

Then a measuring rod like a staff was given to me, and I was told, "Get up and measure the temple of God, and the altar, and the ones who worship there. But do not measure the outer courtyard of the temple; leave it out because it has been given to the Gentiles, and they will trample on the holy city for forty-two months. And I will grant my two witnesses authority to prophesy for 1,260 days, dressed in sackcloth." (These are the two olive trees and the two lampstands that stand before the Lord of the earth.) If anyone wants to harm them, fire comes out of their mouths and completely consumes their enemies. If anyone wants to harm them, they must be killed this way. These two have the power to close up the sky so that it does not rain during the time they are prophesying. They have power to turn the waters to blood and to strike the earth with every kind of plague whenever they want. When they have completed their testimony, the beast that comes up from the abyss will make war on them and conquer them and kill them. Their corpses will lie in the street of the great city that is symbolically called Sodom and Egypt, where their Lord was also crucified. For three and a half days those from every people, tribe, nation, and language will look at their corpses because they will not permit them to be placed in a tomb. And those who live on the earth will rejoice over them and celebrate, even sending gifts to each other because these two prophets had tormented those who live on the earth. But after three and a half days a breath of life from God entered them, and they stood on their feet, and tremendous fear seized those who were watching them. Then they heard a loud voice from heaven saying to them: "Come up here!" So the two prophets went up to heaven in a cloud while their enemies stared at them. Just then a major earthquake took place and a tenth of the city collapsed; seven thousand people were killed in the earthquake, and the rest were terrified and gave glory to the God of heaven.

The second woe has come and gone; the third is coming quickly.

THE SEVENTH TRUMPET

Then the seventh angel blew his trumpet, and there were loud voices in heaven saying:

"The kingdom of the world
has become the kingdom of our Lord
and of his Christ,
and he will reign for ever and ever."

Then the twenty-four elders who are seated on their thrones before God threw themselves down with their faces to the ground and worshiped God with these words:

"We give you thanks, Lord God, the All-Powerful,
the one who is and who was,
because you have taken your great power
and begun to reign.
The nations were enraged,
but your wrath has come,
and the time has come for the dead to be judged,
and the time has come to give to your servants,
the prophets, their reward,
as well as to the saints

and to those who revere your name, both
small and great,
and the time has come to destroy those
who destroy the earth."

Then the temple of God in heaven was opened, and the ark of his covenant was visible within his temple. And there were flashes of lightning, roaring, crashes of thunder, an earthquake, and a great hailstorm.

CHAPTER 12

THE WOMAN, THE CHILD, AND THE DRAGON

Then a great sign appeared in heaven: a woman clothed with the sun, and with the moon under her feet, and on her head was a crown of twelve stars. She was pregnant and was screaming in labor pains, struggling to give birth. Then another sign appeared in heaven: a huge red dragon that had seven heads and ten horns, and on its heads were seven diadem crowns. Now the dragon's tail swept away a third of the stars in heaven and hurled them to the earth. Then the dragon stood before the woman who was about to give birth, so that he might devour her child as soon as it was born. So the woman gave birth to a son, a male child, who is going *to rule over all the nations with an iron rod.* Her child was suddenly caught up to God and to his throne, and she fled into the wilderness where a place had been prepared for her by God, so she could be taken care of for 1,260 days.

WAR IN HEAVEN

Then war broke out in heaven: Michael and his angels fought against the dragon, and the dragon and his angels fought back. But the dragon was not strong enough to prevail, so there was no longer any place left in heaven for him and his angels. So that huge dragon—the ancient serpent, the one called the devil and Satan, who deceives the whole world—was thrown down to the earth, and his angels along with him. Then I heard a loud voice in heaven saying,

"The salvation and the power
and the kingdom of our God,
and the ruling authority of his Christ,
have now come,
because the accuser of our brothers and sisters,
the one who accuses them day and night before our God,
has been thrown down.
But they overcame him
by the blood of the Lamb
and by the word of their testimony,
and they did not love their lives so much that they were afraid to die.
Therefore you heavens rejoice, and all who reside in them!
But woe to the earth and the sea
because the devil has come down to you!
He is filled with terrible anger,
for he knows that he only has a little time!"

Now when the dragon realized that he had been thrown down to the earth, he pursued the woman who had given birth to the male child. But the woman was given the two wings of a giant eagle so that she could fly out into the wilderness, to the place God prepared for her, where she is taken care of—away from the presence of the serpent—for a time, times, and half a time. Then the serpent spouted water like a river out of his mouth after the woman in an attempt to sweep her away by a flood, but the earth came to her rescue; the ground opened up and swallowed the river that the dragon had spewed from his mouth. So the dragon became enraged at the woman and went away to make war on the rest of her children, those who keep God's commandments and hold to the testimony about Jesus. And the dragon stood on the sand of the seashore.

CHAPTER 13

THE TWO BEASTS

Then I saw a beast coming up out of the sea. It had ten horns and seven heads, and on its horns were ten diadem crowns, and on its heads a blasphemous name. Now the beast that I saw was like a leopard, but its feet were like a bear's, and its mouth was like a lion's mouth. The dragon gave the beast his power, his throne, and great authority to rule. One of the beast's heads appeared to have been killed, but the lethal wound had been healed. And the whole world followed the beast in amazement; they worshiped the dragon because he had given ruling authority to the beast, and they worshiped the beast too, saying: "Who is like the beast?" and "Who is able to make war against him?" The beast was given a mouth speaking proud words and blasphemies, and he was permitted to exercise ruling authority for forty-two months. So the beast opened his mouth to blaspheme against God—to blaspheme both his name and his dwelling place, that is, those who dwell in heaven. The beast was permitted to go to war against the saints and conquer them. He was given ruling authority over every tribe, people, language, and nation, and all those who live on the earth will worship the beast, everyone whose name has not been written since the foundation of the world in the book of life belonging to the Lamb who was killed. If anyone has an ear, he had better listen!

> If anyone is meant for captivity,
> into captivity he will go.
> If anyone is to be killed by the sword,
> then by the sword he must be killed.

This requires steadfast endurance and faith from the saints.

Then I saw another beast coming up from the earth. He had two horns like a lamb, but was speaking like a dragon. He exercised all the ruling authority of the first beast on his behalf, and made the earth and those who inhabit it worship the first beast, the one whose lethal wound had been healed. He performed momentous signs, even making fire come down from heaven to earth in front of people and, by the signs he was permitted to perform on behalf of the beast, he deceived those who live on the earth. He told those who live on the earth to make an image to the beast who had been wounded by the sword, but still lived. The second beast was empowered to give life to the image of the first beast so that it could speak, and could cause all those who did not worship the image of the beast to be killed. He also caused everyone (small and great, rich and poor, free and slave) to obtain a mark on their right hand or on their forehead. Thus no one was allowed to buy or sell things unless he bore the mark of the beast—that is, his name or his number. This calls for wisdom: Let the one who has insight calculate the beast's number, for it is man's number, and his number is 666.

CHAPTER 14

AN INTERLUDE: THE SONG OF THE 144,000

Then I looked, and here was the Lamb standing on Mount Zion, and with him were 144,000, who had his name and his Father's name written on their foreheads. I also heard a sound coming out of heaven like the sound of many waters and like the sound of loud thunder. Now the sound I heard was like that made by harpists playing their harps, and they were singing a new song before the throne and before the four living creatures and the elders. No one was able to learn the song except the 144,000 who had been redeemed from the earth.

These are the ones who have not defiled themselves with women, for they are virgins. These are the ones who follow the Lamb wherever he goes. These were redeemed from humanity as firstfruits to God and to the Lamb, and no lie was found on their lips; they are blameless.

THREE ANGELS AND THREE MESSAGES

Then I saw another angel flying directly overhead, and he had an eternal gospel to proclaim to those who live on the earth—to every nation, tribe, language, and people. He declared in a loud voice: "Fear God and give him glory because the hour of his judgment has arrived, and worship the one who made heaven and earth, the sea and the springs of water!"

A second angel followed the first, declaring: "Fallen, fallen is Babylon the great city! She made all the nations drink of the wine of her immoral passion."

A third angel followed the first two, declaring in a loud voice: "If anyone worships the beast and his image, and takes the mark on his forehead or his hand, that person will also drink of the wine of God's anger that has been mixed undiluted in the cup of his wrath, and he will be tortured with fire and sulfur in front of the holy angels and in front of the Lamb. And the smoke from their torture will go up forever and ever, and those who worship the beast and his image will have no rest day or night, along with anyone who receives the mark of his name." This requires the steadfast endurance of the saints—those who obey God's commandments and hold to their faith in Jesus.

Then I heard a voice from heaven say, "Write this:

'Blessed are the dead,
those who die in the Lord from this
moment on!' "

"Yes," says the Spirit, "so they can rest from their hard work, because their deeds will follow them."

Then I looked, and a white cloud appeared, and seated *on the cloud was one like a son of man!* He had a golden crown on his head and a sharp sickle in his hand. Then another angel came out of the temple, shouting in a loud voice to the one seated on the cloud, "Use your sickle and start to reap, because the time to reap has come, since the earth's harvest is ripe!" So the one seated on the cloud swung his sickle over the earth, and the earth was reaped.

Then another angel came out of the temple in heaven, and he, too, had a sharp sickle. Another angel, who was in charge of the fire, came from the altar and called in a loud voice to the angel who had the sharp sickle, "Use your sharp sickle and gather the clusters of grapes off the vine of the earth, because its grapes are now ripe." So the angel swung his sickle over the earth and gathered the grapes from the vineyard of the earth and tossed them into the great winepress of the wrath of God. Then the winepress was stomped outside the city, and blood poured out of the winepress up to the height of horses' bridles for a distance of almost 200 miles.

CHAPTER 15

THE FINAL PLAGUES

Then I saw another great and astounding sign in heaven: seven angels who have seven final plagues (they are final because in them God's anger is completed).

Then I saw something like a sea of glass mixed with fire, and those who had conquered the beast and his image and the number of his name. They were standing by the sea of glass, holding harps given to them by God. They sang the song of Moses the servant of God and the song of the Lamb:

"Great and astounding are your deeds,
Lord God, the All-Powerful!
Just and true are your ways,
King over the nations!
Who will not fear you, O Lord,
and glorify your name, because you alone
are holy?
All nations will come and worship
before you
for your righteous acts have been revealed."

After these things I looked, and the temple (the tent of the testimony) was opened in heaven, and the seven angels who had the seven plagues came out of the temple, dressed in clean bright linen, wearing wide golden belts around their chests. Then one of the four living creatures gave the seven angels seven golden bowls filled with the wrath of God who lives forever and ever, and the temple was filled with smoke from God's glory and from his power. Thus no one could enter the temple until the seven plagues from the seven angels were completed.

CHAPTER 16

THE BOWLS OF GOD'S WRATH

Then I heard a loud voice from the temple declaring to the seven angels: "Go and pour out on the earth the seven bowls containing God's wrath." So the first angel went and poured out his bowl on the earth. Then ugly and painful sores appeared on the people who had the mark of the beast and who worshiped his image.

Next, the second angel poured out his bowl on the sea, and it turned into blood, like that of a corpse, and every living creature that was in the sea died.

Then the third angel poured out his bowl on the rivers and the springs of water, and they turned into blood. Now I heard the angel of the waters saying:

"You are just—the one who is and who was,

the Holy One—because you have passed
these judgments,
because they poured out the blood of
your saints and prophets,
so you have given them blood to drink.
They got what they deserved!"

Then I heard the altar reply, "Yes, Lord God, the All-Powerful, your judgments are true and just!"

Then the fourth angel poured out his bowl on the sun, and it was permitted to scorch people with fire. Thus people were scorched by the terrible heat, yet they blasphemed the name of God, who has ruling authority over these plagues, and they would not repent and give him glory.

Then the fifth angel poured out his bowl on the throne of the beast so that darkness covered his kingdom, and people began to bite their tongues because of their pain. They blasphemed the God of heaven because of their sufferings and because of their sores, but nevertheless they still refused to repent of their deeds.

Then the sixth angel poured out his bowl on the great river Euphrates and dried up its water to prepare the way for the kings from the east. Then I saw three unclean spirits that looked like frogs coming out of the mouth of the dragon, out of the mouth of the beast, and out of the mouth of the false prophet. For they are the spirits of the demons performing signs who go out to the kings of the earth to bring them together for the battle that will take place on the great day of God, the All-Powerful.

(Look! I will come like a thief!
Blessed is the one who stays alert and does not lose his clothes so that he will not have to walk around naked and his shameful condition be seen.)

Now the spirits gathered the kings and their armies to the place that is called Armageddon in Hebrew.

Finally the seventh angel poured out his bowl into the air and a loud voice came out of the temple from the throne, saying: "It is done!" Then there were flashes of lightning, roaring, and crashes of thunder, and there was a tremendous earthquake—an earthquake unequaled since humanity has been on the earth, so tremendous was that earthquake. The great city was split into three parts, and the cities of the nations collapsed. So Babylon the great was remembered before God and was given the cup filled with the wine made of God's furious wrath. Every island fled away, and no mountains could be found. And gigantic hailstones, weighing about a 100 pounds each, fell from heaven on people, but they blasphemed God because of the plague of hail, since it was so horrendous.

CHAPTER 17

THE GREAT PROSTITUTE AND THE BEAST

Then one of the seven angels who had the seven bowls came and spoke to me. "Come," he said, "I will show you the condemnation and punishment of the great prostitute who sits on many waters, with whom the kings of the earth committed sexual immorality and the earth's inhabitants got drunk with the wine of her immorality." So he carried me away in the Spirit to a wilderness, and there I saw a woman sitting on a scarlet beast that was full of blasphemous names and had seven heads and ten horns. Now the woman was dressed in purple and scarlet clothing, and adorned with gold, precious stones, and pearls. She held in her hand a golden cup filled with detestable things and unclean things from her sexual immorality. On her forehead was written a name, a mystery: "Babylon the Great, the Mother of prostitutes and of the detestable things of the earth." I saw that the woman was drunk with the blood of the saints and the blood of those who testified to Jesus. I was greatly astounded when I saw her. But the angel said to me, "Why are you astounded? I will interpret for you the mystery of the woman and of the beast with the seven heads and ten horns that carries her. The beast you saw was, and is not, but is about to come up from the abyss and then go to destruction. The inhabitants of the earth—all those whose names have not been written in the book of life since the foundation of the world—will be astounded when they see that the beast was, and is not, but is to come. (This requires a mind that has wisdom.) The seven heads are seven mountains the woman sits on. They are also seven kings: five have fallen; one is, and the other has not yet come, but whenever he does come, he must remain for only a brief time. The beast that was, and is not, is himself an eighth king and yet is one of the seven, and is going to destruction. The ten horns that you saw are ten kings who have not yet received a kingdom, but will receive ruling authority as kings with the beast for one hour. These kings have a single intent, and they will give their power and authority to the beast. They will make war with the Lamb, but the Lamb will conquer them, because he is Lord of lords and King of kings, and those accompanying the Lamb are the called, chosen, and faithful."

Then the angel said to me, "The waters you saw (where the prostitute is seated) are peoples, multitudes, nations, and languages. The ten horns that you saw, and the beast—these will hate the prostitute and make her desolate and naked. They will consume her flesh and burn her up with fire. For God has put into their minds to carry out his purpose by making a decision to give their royal power to the beast until the words of God are fulfilled. As for the woman you saw, she is the great city that has sovereignty over the kings of the earth."

CHAPTER 18

BABYLON IS DESTROYED

After these things I saw another angel, who possessed great authority, coming down out of heaven, and the earth was lit up by his radiance. He shouted with a powerful voice:

"Fallen, fallen, is Babylon the great!
She has become a lair for demons,
a haunt for every unclean spirit,
a haunt for every unclean bird,
a haunt for every unclean and detested beast.
For all the nations have fallen from
the wine of her immoral passion,
and the kings of the earth have committed sexual immorality with her,
and the merchants of the earth have gotten rich from the power of her sensual behavior."

Then I heard another voice from heaven saying, "Come out of her, my people, so you will not take part in her sins and so you will not receive her plagues, because her sins have piled up all the way to heaven and God has remembered her crimes. Repay her the same way she repaid others; pay her back double corresponding to her deeds. In the cup she mixed, mix double the amount for her. As much as she exalted herself and lived in sensual luxury, to this extent give her torment and grief because she said to herself, 'I rule as queen and am no widow; I will never experience grief!' For this reason, she will experience her plagues in a single day: disease, mourning, and famine, and she will be burned down with fire, because the Lord God who judges her is powerful!"

Then the kings of the earth who committed immoral acts with her and lived in sensual luxury with her will weep and wail for her when they see the smoke from the fire that burns her up. They will stand a long way off because they are afraid of her torment, and will say,

"Woe, woe, O great city,
Babylon the powerful city!
For in a single hour your doom has come!"

Then the merchants of the earth will weep and mourn for her because no one buys their cargo any longer—cargo such as gold, silver, precious stones, pearls, fine linen, purple cloth, silk, scarlet cloth, all sorts of things made of citron wood, all sorts of objects made of ivory, all sorts of things made of expensive wood, bronze, iron and marble, cinnamon, spice, incense, perfumed ointment, frankincense, wine, olive oil and costly flour, wheat, cattle and sheep, horses and four-wheeled carriages, slaves and human lives.

(The ripe fruit you greatly desired
has gone from you,
and all your luxury and splendor
have gone from you—
they will never ever be found again!)

The merchants who sold these things, who got rich from her, will stand a long way off because they are afraid of her torment. They will weep and mourn, saying,

"Woe, woe, O great city—
dressed in fine linen, purple and scarlet
clothing,

and adorned with gold, precious stones,
and pearls—
because in a single hour such great
wealth has been destroyed!"

And every ship's captain, and all who sail along the coast—seamen, and all who make their living from the sea, stood a long way off and began to shout when they saw the smoke from the fire that burned her up, "Who is like the great city?" And they threw dust on their heads and were shouting with weeping and mourning,

"Woe, Woe, O great city—
in which all those who had ships on the
sea got rich from her wealth—
because in a single hour she has been
destroyed!"
(Rejoice over her, O heaven,
and you saints and apostles and prophets,
for God has pronounced judgment
against her on your behalf!)

Then one powerful angel picked up a stone like a huge millstone, threw it into the sea, and said,

"With this kind of sudden violent force
Babylon the great city will be thrown
down,
and it will never be found again!
And the sound of the harpists,
musicians,
flute players, and trumpeters
will never be heard in you again.

No craftsman who practices any trade
will ever be found in you again;
the noise of a mill will never be heard in
you again.
Even the light from a lamp
will never shine in you again!
The voices of the bridegroom and his bride
will never be heard in you again.
For your merchants were the tycoons of
the world,
because all the nations were deceived by
your magic spells!
The blood of the saints and prophets was
found in her,
along with the blood of all those who had
been killed on the earth."

CHAPTER 19

After these things I heard what sounded like the loud voice of a vast throng in heaven, saying,

"Hallelujah! Salvation and glory and
power belong to our God,
because his judgments are true and just.
For he has judged the great prostitute
who corrupted the earth with her sexual
immorality,
and has avenged the blood of his servants
poured out by her own hands!"

Then a second time the crowd shouted, "Hallelujah!" The smoke rises from her forever and ever. The twenty-four elders and the four living creatures threw themselves to the ground and worshiped God, who was seated on the throne, saying: "Amen! Hallelujah!"

Then a voice came from the throne, saying:

"Praise our God
all you his servants,
and all you who fear him,
both the small and the great!"

THE WEDDING CELEBRATION OF THE LAMB

Then I heard what sounded like the voice of a vast throng, like the roar of many waters and like loud crashes of thunder. They were shouting:

"Hallelujah!
For the Lord our God, the All-Powerful, reigns!
Let us rejoice and exult
and give him glory,
because the wedding celebration of the Lamb has come,
and his bride has made herself ready.
She was permitted to be dressed in bright, clean, fine linen" (for the fine linen is the righteous deeds of the saints).

Then the angel said to me, "Write the following: Blessed are those who are invited to the banquet at the wedding celebration of the Lamb!" He also said to me, "These are the true words of God." So I threw myself down at his feet to worship him, but he said, "Do not do this! I am only a fellow servant with you and your brothers and sisters who hold to the testimony about Jesus. Worship God, for the testimony about Jesus is the spirit of prophecy."

THE SON OF GOD GOES TO WAR

Then I saw heaven opened and here came a white horse! The one riding it was called "Faithful" and "True," and with justice he judges and goes to war. His eyes are like a fiery flame and there are many diadem crowns on his head. He has a name written that no one knows except himself. He is dressed in clothing dipped in blood, and he is called the Word of God. The armies that are in heaven, dressed in white, clean, fine linen, were following him on white horses. From his mouth extends a sharp sword so that with it he can strike the nations. ***He will rule them with an iron rod,*** and he stomps the winepress of the furious wrath of God, the All-Powerful. He has a name written on his clothing and on his thigh: "King of kings and Lord of lords."

Then I saw one angel standing in the sun, and he shouted in a loud voice to all the birds flying high in the sky:

"Come, gather around for the great
  banquet of God,
to eat your fill of the flesh of kings,
the flesh of generals,
the flesh of powerful people,
the flesh of horses and those who ride
  them,
and the flesh of all people, both free and
  slave,
and small and great!"

Then I saw the beast and the kings of the earth and their armies assembled to do battle with the one who rode the horse and with his army. Now the beast was seized, and along with him the false prophet who had performed the signs on his behalf—signs by which he deceived those who had received the mark of the beast and those who worshiped his image. Both of them were thrown alive into the lake of fire burning with sulfur. The others were killed by the sword that extended from the mouth of the one who rode the horse, and all the birds gorged themselves with their flesh.

CHAPTER 20

THE THOUSAND-YEAR REIGN

Then I saw an angel descending from heaven, holding in his hand the key to the abyss and a huge chain. He seized the dragon—the ancient serpent, who is the devil and Satan—and tied him up for a thousand years. The angel then threw him into the abyss and locked and sealed it so that he could not deceive the nations until the one thousand years were finished. (After these things he must be released for a brief period of time.)

Then I saw thrones and seated on them were those who had been given authority to judge. I also saw the souls of those who had been beheaded because of the testimony about Jesus and because of the word of God. These had not worshiped the beast or his image and had refused to receive his mark on their forehead or hand. They came to life and reigned with Christ for a thousand years. (The rest of the dead did not come to life until the thousand years were finished.) This is the first resurrection. Blessed and holy is the one who takes part in the first resurrection. The second death has no power over them, but they will be priests of God and of Christ, and they will reign with him for a thousand years.

SATAN'S FINAL DEFEAT

Now when the thousand years are finished, Satan will be released from his prison and will go out to deceive the nations at the four corners of the earth, Gog and Magog, to bring them together for the battle. They are as numerous as the grains of sand in the sea. They went up on the broad plain of the earth and encircled the camp of the saints and the beloved city, but fire came down from heaven and devoured them completely. And the devil who deceived them was thrown into the lake of fire and sulfur, where the beast and the false prophet are too, and they will be tormented there day and night forever and ever.

THE GREAT WHITE THRONE

Then I saw a large white throne and the one who was seated on it; the earth and the heaven fled from his presence, and no place was found for them. And I saw the dead, the great and the small, standing before the throne. Then books were opened, and another book was opened—the book of life. So the dead were judged by what was written in the books, according to their deeds. The sea gave up the dead that were in it, and Death and Hades gave up the dead that were in them, and each one was judged according to his deeds. Then Death and Hades were thrown into the lake of fire. This is the second death—the lake of fire. If anyone's name was not found written in the book of life, that person was thrown into the lake of fire.

CHAPTER 21

A NEW HEAVEN AND A NEW EARTH

Then I saw a new heaven and a new earth, for the first heaven and earth had ceased to exist, and the sea existed no more. And I saw the holy city—the new Jerusalem—descending out of heaven from God, made ready like a bride adorned for her husband. And I heard a loud voice from the throne saying: "Look! The residence of God is among human beings. He will live among them, and they will be his people, and God himself will be with them. He will wipe away every tear from their eyes, and death will not exist any more—or mourning, or crying, or pain, for the former things have ceased to exist."

And the one seated on the throne said: "Look! I am making all things new!" Then he said to me, "Write it down, because these words are reliable and true." He also said to me, "It is done! I am the Alpha and the Omega, the beginning and the end. To the one who is thirsty I will give water free of charge from the spring of the water of life. The one who conquers will inherit these things, and I will be his God and he will be my son. But as for the cowards, unbelievers, detestable persons, murderers, the sexually immoral, and those who practice magic spells, idol worshipers, and all those who lie, their place will be in the lake that burns with fire and sulfur. That is the second death."

THE NEW JERUSALEM DESCENDS

Then one of the seven angels who had the seven bowls full of the seven final plagues came and spoke to me, saying, "Come, I will show you the bride, the wife of the Lamb!" So he took me away in the Spirit to a huge, majestic mountain and showed me the holy city, Jerusalem, descending out of heaven from God. The city possesses the glory of God; its brilliance is like a precious jewel, like a stone of crystal-clear jasper. It has a massive, high wall with twelve gates, with twelve angels at the gates, and the names of the twelve tribes of the nation of Israel are written on the gates. There are three gates on the east side, three gates on the north side, three gates on the south side, and three gates on the west side. The wall of the city has twelve foundations, and on them are the twelve names of the twelve apostles of the Lamb.

The angel who spoke to me had a golden measuring rod with which to measure the city and its foundation stones and wall. Now the city is laid out as a square, its length and width the same. He measured the city with the measuring rod at 1,400 miles (its length and width and height are equal). He also measured its wall, 144 cubits according to human measurement, which is also the angel's. The city's wall is made of jasper and the city is pure gold, like transparent glass. The foundations of the city's wall are decorated with every kind of precious stone. The first foundation is jasper, the second sapphire, the third agate, the fourth emerald, the fifth onyx, the sixth carnelian, the seventh chrysolite, the eighth beryl, the ninth topaz, the tenth chrysoprase, the eleventh jacinth, and the twelfth amethyst. And the twelve gates are twelve pearls—each one of the gates is made from just one pearl! The main street of the city is pure gold, like transparent glass.

Now I saw no temple in the city, because the Lord God—the All-Powerful—and the Lamb are its temple. The city does not need the sun or the moon to shine on it, because the glory of God lights it up, and its lamp is the Lamb. The nations will walk by its light, and the kings of the earth will bring their grandeur into it. Its gates will never be closed during the day (and there will be no night there). They will bring the grandeur and the wealth of the nations into it, but nothing ritually unclean will ever enter into it, nor anyone who does what is detestable or practices falsehood, but only those whose names are written in the Lamb's book of life.

CHAPTER 22

Then the angel showed me the river of the water of life—water as clear as crystal—pouring out from the throne of God and of the Lamb, flowing down the middle of the city's main street. On each side of the river is the tree of life producing 12 kinds of fruit, yielding its fruit every month of the year. Its leaves are for the healing of the nations. And there will no longer be any curse, and the throne of God and the Lamb will be in the city. His servants will worship him, and they will see his face, and his name will be on their foreheads. Night will be no more, and they will not need the light of a lamp or the light of the sun, because the Lord God will shine on them, and they will reign forever and ever.

A FINAL REMINDER

Then the angel said to me, "These words are reliable and true. The Lord, the God of the spirits of the prophets, has sent his angel to show his servants what must happen soon."

(Look! I am coming soon!
Blessed is the one who keeps the words of the prophecy expressed in this book.)

I, John, am the one who heard and saw these things, and when I heard and saw them, I threw myself down to worship at the feet of the angel who was showing them to me. But he said to me, "Do not do this! I am a fellow servant with you and with your brothers the prophets, and with those who obey the words of this book. Worship God!" Then he said to me, "Do not seal up the words of the prophecy contained in this book, because the time is near. The evildoer must continue to do evil, and the one who is morally filthy must continue to be filthy. The one who is righteous must continue to act righteously, and the one who is holy must continue to be holy."

(Look! I am coming soon,
and my reward is with me to pay each
one according to what he has done!
I am the Alpha and the Omega,
the first and the last,
the beginning and the end!)

Blessed are those who wash their robes so they can have access to the tree of life and can enter into the city by the gates. Outside are the dogs and the sorcerers and the sexually immoral, and the murderers, and the idolaters and everyone who loves and practices falsehood!

"I, Jesus, have sent my angel to testify to you about these things for the churches. I am the root and the descendant of David, the bright morning star!" And the Spirit and the bride say, "Come!" And let the one who hears say: "Come!" And let the one who is thirsty come; let the one who wants it take the water of life free of charge.

I testify to everyone who hears the words of the prophecy contained in this book: If anyone adds to them, God will add to him the plagues described in this book. And if anyone takes away from the words of this book of prophecy, God will take away his share in the tree of life and in the holy city that are described in this book.

The one who testifies to these things says, "Yes, I am coming soon!" Amen! Come, Lord Jesus! The grace of the Lord Jesus be with all.